# Playing on High Ground

## A Christian Approach to the Mental Game

## Ray Santiago III, MK

Linds – God Bless – Sure love you + thankful for your life + faithful stand for the 1 true God. May this book encourage you to continue to learn + live + give God's Word to the world much love in Christ –

Playing on High Ground
A Christian Approach to the Mental Game
©2017 by Ray Santiago III, MK

ISBN: 978-1548070717

# What Others Are Saying About
## *Playing on High Ground*

"This book is awesome! I read the first chapter before a game this season and, to be honest, I had been struggling the previous 2 months with walks... almost as bad as having the yips. That night I was able to just believe in myself and that God would take care of me. I felt like the apostle Peter in Chapter 1 in the storm and flipped the switch. I started believing! Performance aside, the first chapter alone taught me to always believe. I felt like the main character Jacoby. My reading has been pretty lacking as of late. Today showed me how much God can help if you let Him."

-*Caleb Frare*
*NY Yankees Prospect*


"The way the mental game and a relationship with Christ is intertwined is remarkable. Something I wish I had considered while I played: "but when you elevate your thinking to God's perfect thoughts, it takes self-talk to much higher ground." While playing, I used self talk every day. Had I used God's perfect Word, it would've been that much better. I am not perfect, my words are not perfect, but His are. I tried to make my play as perfect as I could, in an imperfect game. Using His words... WOW!"

-*Kyle Johnson*
*Former MLB Prospect and Current Owner of BigLeagueLocker.com*


"*Playing on High Ground* is an excellent resource for the Christian competitor or coach. If you want an engaging way to discover what the Bible says about playing at your peak with true purpose, then read this book. It will take you to higher ground."

-*Gina Parris*
*Speaker & Performance Coach, BuiltToWin.com*

# Acknowledgements

*I am thankful to God and His Son Jesus Christ for all they've done for me in giving me life and giving it to me more than abundantly.*

*To my family (Ray, Linda, Rory, Lex, Katelynn, Grandma Sue) and to my friends, who have supported me throughout my life and during the patient writing process.*

*To my Grandma Gloria, who exemplifies a lifetime of loving service.*

*I am also thankful to those who've gone before me to teach me God's Word rightly divided and to the men and women who have represented the field of Sport Psychology with integrity.*

# Preface

*Playing on High Ground* is a book for athletes desiring to grow in their relationship with God and improve their mental game in order to give their all for the one who gave his life for all, Jesus Christ.

The motivation behind this book was first and foremost to share God's Word with the world, and secondly to equip Christian athletes with examples God chose to place in His Word for our learning and sharing so that all men might be saved and come unto a knowledge of the Truth (1 Timothy 2:3-4).

In this book you'll find that God's Word is chock-full of great examples of ordinary people doing extraordinary things because they *believed* in an extraordinary God. May their examples of believing encourage you to persevere with purpose as you pursue your athletic dreams, always remaining in anticipation of the surest hope we have, which is the return of Jesus Christ![1]

---

[1] **Romans 15:4 WT**: Moreover, whatever was written previously was written for our teaching, so that through the patient endurance and through the encouragement of the Scriptures we might have the hope.

**At the completion of this book my hope is threefold**:

- That you would **learn** God's Word and develop a greater appetite for consistently reading, studying, and applying the Scriptures in your life.

- That you would **live** God's Word in your heart, mind, speech, and actions shining as a light in a dark world.[2]

- That you would be prepared in season and out of season to **give** the Words of life to others when they see you evidencing the love of God and ask the reason for the hope that is in you.[3]

Although this book has a baseball theme, it is applicable to all performers desiring to grow with God and praise Him through their performance. The following story is fictional and not based on anyone in particular, but the Scriptures are as real and alive as when God first had them written down.[4]

---

[2] **Philippians 2:15-16 ESV®**: [15]that you may be blameless and innocent, children of God without blemish in the midst of a crooked and twisted generation, among whom you shine as lights in the world, [16]holding fast to the word of life, so that in the day of Christ I may be proud that I did not run in vain or labor in vain.

[3] **1 Peter 3:15 NIV®**: But in your hearts revere Christ as Lord. Always be prepared to give an answer to everyone who asks you to give the reason for the hope that you have. But do this with gentleness and respect,

[4] **Hebrews 4:12 ESV®**: For the word of God is living and active, sharper than any two-edged sword, piercing to the division of soul and of spirit, of joints and of marrow, and discerning the thoughts and intentions of the heart.

# Introduction

Jacoby Johnson is a high school senior in southern California who's earned a Division One scholarship to play baseball and who has impressed scouts enough to consider drafting him in next month's Major League Baseball June Draft.

With his baseball stock rising, Jacoby finds himself spending less time attending Church and more time playing scout ball each weekend. Since five years old playing baseball is all he's ever wanted to do and now, comfortable with a scholarship and a chance at getting drafted, his future seems bright with all his hard work paying off.

While throwing in the 7$^{th}$ inning of a game late in the high school season, Jacoby feels a sharp pain in his elbow after delivering a pitch. After being examined by his coach and trainer, he's sent to the Emergency Room for an MRI. The results confirm a tear in his UCL (Ulnar Collateral Ligament) requiring Tommy John surgery on his elbow and a one-year recovery. Jacoby's world seemingly comes crashing down. No baseball meant no life.

On the day of the surgery, the surgeon, a former baseball player, walks in to tell Jacoby a bit more about the procedure and finds his parents praying for him in the waiting room. After a successful surgery, the surgeon recommends to Jacoby that he meet with a Sport Psychologist friend of his named Dr. Marcus Mack, who helped him mentally get through injuries as well as grow in his relationship with God. Somewhat reluctant to be associated with a *mental coach*, Jacoby agrees to one meeting.

In the following story you'll watch the relationship between Jacoby and Dr. Marcus Mack grow as Jacoby learns to make the best of his time away from the game.

# God Confidence

## Chapter 1

I arrived at my session with Dr. Marcus Mack a few minutes early and looked around to make sure no one saw me, the best baseball player in the area, meeting with a psychologist to talk about my feelings. Entering his office building I was greeted by a hallway covered in signed pictures of local and professional athletes, with one in particular catching my eye that read, "Thanks, Mack. In God We Trust!"

Just then, an athletic-looking man about my height at six feet tall, wearing a light blue collared shirt, approached me with a warm smile. "You must be Jacoby."

"Yes. Are you Dr. Mack?" I asked while shaking his hand.

"That's me. Good to meet you. Feel free to look around. I'll be with you in a moment."

As I returned to browsing the photos and memorabilia, I couldn't help but replay my elbow injury and worry how upset my college coach will be to hear I got injured. I thought of all the people I was letting down and the fun I'd be missing with buddies playing summer ball. What was I going to do without baseball? How could this happen to *me*?

"Jacoby, I'm ready for you," he said emerging from his office and waking me from my nightmare.

More signed pictures of him with athletes and their favorite Bible verses lined the walls of his office. "I was told you work with a lot of Christian athletes on their mental game. I'm Christian. Well, I say I'm Christian but I haven't been to Church in a while and my prayer life is off and on. Usually I just call on the Big Guy when I need something."

"I don't think you're alone in that category," Mack said encouragingly. "And yes, some of my clients ask me to share how they can grow in their relationship with God to help handle the highs and lows that life and sport so often bring. But I enjoy working with all athletes and making sure they know someone cares more about the name on the back of their jersey than the number."

Telling from the pictures around his office, I got a good sense it was true. "So what exactly do you do with athletes, Dr. Mack?"

"Most people call me Coach or Mack. You can call me either one," he said. "To answer your question, as a Sport Psychologist my first priority, no matter who I'm working with, is to listen. Sometimes the thing an athlete needs most is just to vent and be heard. Once I get a better understanding of what they're experiencing, I introduce them to mental strategies like routine building, emotion management systems, positive self-talk, and imagery to help them perform with confidence and allow their bodies to do what they've trained them to do."

I had heard of Sport Psychology before but thought it was more for athletes who were struggling. I had never experienced failure and didn't see a need for working on my mental game at that point. "I'm sure it works for some people but I don't think it's for me. Out of curiosity, how does it differ when you work with Christian athletes?"

"We discuss the same mental strategies for building *self*-confidence on the field but we also make time to pray and open the Bible together to build a *God* confidence off the field. **In sport, the better you understand yourself, the more confidence you'll have in your ability to respond well in the heat of competition**. **In life, the better you know God's**

**ability, the more confident you'll be in approaching Him when things seem to be falling apart**," he stated.

"Is there a difference between building *confidence* through Sport Psychology and *believing* in God?" I asked.

"In some ways they're similar and in others they're quite different. I like to share the account of Peter walking on water to show the similarities and differences. Would you like to check it out?"

"I guess so," I answered, somewhat interested.

Mack walked to a big bookshelf and retrieved two Bibles, handing me one. It almost felt foreign to be reading a Bible outside of Church, and actually, to be reading one at all.

As he sat back down and started flipping towards the back end of his Bible he said, "Alright, let's turn to the gospel of Matthew, where we'll pick it up right after Jesus had miraculously fed over 5,000 people on a few fishes and loaves – *no big deal*," he said with a wink. "Starting in chapter 14 verse 22 it says,

Matthew 14:22-29[NIV®]

[22]Immediately Jesus made the disciples get into the boat and go on ahead of him to the other side, while he dismissed the crowd.

[23]After he had dismissed them, he went up on a mountainside by himself to pray. Later that night, he was there alone,

[24]and the boat was already a considerable distance from land, buffeted by the waves because the wind was against it.

[25]Shortly before dawn Jesus went out to them, walking on the lake.

[26]When the disciples saw him walking on the lake, they were terrified. "It's a ghost," they said, and cried out in fear.

[27]But Jesus immediately said to them: "Take courage! It is I. Don't be afraid."

[28]"Lord, if it's you," Peter replied, "tell me to come to you on the water."

[29]"Come," he said. Then Peter got down out of the boat, walked on the water and came toward Jesus.

"Now, let's pause here for a second to consider the situation," Mack said to recap. "Here Jesus' disciples are getting tossed around by the wind and waves and they see a figure walking on water towards them. We'd probably be a little freaked out too! Yet, Jesus reassures them and calmly tells them to be courageous rather than fearful. And Peter, often willing to put his foot in his mouth, says, *If it's really you, Jesus, tell me to come out there.* And what was Jesus' response?"

"Come."

"So Peter went below deck, put his Beats by Dre headphones on and blasted *Jock Jams* to get psyched up while visualizing himself walking on water and repeating, 'Float like Jesus on top of the sea. Float like Jesus. I believe in *me*,' until he felt confident enough to do it, right?"

I started laughing. "Well, it doesn't say that but that would've been funny. It says he got out of the boat and walked on the water towards Jesus."

"And *that's* the difference between Sport Psychology and believing God's Word. Sport Psychology is all about developing *self*-confidence through several helpful strategies that *may* lead to success, whereas with God's Word you're believing information backed by God that always succeeds because He cannot fail His Word.[5] Does that make sense?"

"It does. I'm guessing there aren't any Bible verses that promise being Christian will make you a better athlete, right?"

"That would be nice but I haven't found any," Mack said in a joking manner. "But there are plenty of benefits to having a relationship with God that can help along the way as you hone your skills to be the best athlete possible. Let's reread verses 28 and 29 and continue on, as there are some similarities between confidence and believing that are worth noting:

Verses 28-33[NIV®]

[28]"Lord, if it's you," Peter replied, "tell me to come to you on the water."

[29]"Come," he said. Then Peter got down out of the boat, walked on the water and came toward Jesus.

[30]But when he saw the wind, he was afraid and, beginning to sink, cried out, "Lord, save me!"

---

[5] **Numbers 23:19 ESV®**: God is not man, that he should lie, or a son of man, that he should change his mind. Has he said, and will he not do it? Or has he spoken, and will he not fulfill it?

$^{31}$Immediately Jesus reached out his hand and caught him. "You of little faith," he said, "why did you doubt?"

$^{32}$And when they climbed into the boat, the wind died down.

$^{33}$Then those who were in the boat worshiped him, saying, "Truly you are the Son of God."

Mack took a sip of water before continuing, "So we've got Peter walking on water, believingly doing what no man's ever done besides Jesus *and then* he starts looking around at the wind and waves and... and... he starts to doubt what Jesus told him. What failed, Jacoby? The information to walk on water or his believing of that information?"

"His believing."

"That's right. Remember, God's Word cannot fail but we can fail to remain steadfast in our believing of it," he pointed out. "And this is where believing in God and self-confidence share a similar quality in how they work. **Both take a moment-by-moment decision in the mind to maintain, with the main difference being that believing God's Word guarantees success whereas self-confidence doesn't always lead to the desired outcome. Fear and**

**believing can't live in your mind at the same time, as fear is the enemy of believing. You're either going to do one or the other**."

That made sense as I recalled outings on the mound when things were going great until one error or bad call by the umpire caused that little inkling of doubt to crack the door to my mind and, if left unchecked, fear often kicked the door down, resulting in poor performances.

Mack then asked, "When Peter was sinking in fear, Jesus sat there laughing at him with the other guys in the boat and let him suffer for awhile, right?"

I had to admit I liked Mack's sense of humor and sarcasm already. "It says Jesus *immediately* helped him when he called out."

"Just checking," he said. "Peter might have needed some maturing in his believing but he did the absolute right thing in calling out to Jesus for rescue. By the way, how do you think Peter got back to the boat?"

"Well, I don't think Jesus carried him back, so I'm guessing he regained his believing and walked back on his own."

"I think so, too.  Again, **both believing God's Word and *self*-confidence on the field are a moment-by-moment choice and they're only ever a thought away**," he reminded me.

"So when it comes to believing, if there's only two choices – to believe God's Word or not – then why did Jesus call Peter's believing *little*?" I asked.

"Good question.  He was referring to how quickly Peter allowed his surroundings to steer him into doubting Jesus' instructions to 'come.'  *That's* where he had plenty of room to grow in his believing.  In sport, the ability to remain confident when all around you seems to be going against you will prove how fragile or strong your confidence is."

"I see."

"I should also point out that all the *self*-confidence in the world wouldn't have helped Peter walk on water.  Only believing the information from Jesus could give him that ability.  On the flip side, in sport believing in Jesus Christ won't keep errors or bad innings from happening.  That stuff just happens.  How you've mentally prepared yourself to respond to those negatives will be what gets you *back to the boat* or *keeps you sinking*, so to speak," he said with a smile.  "Listen,

Jacoby, I know you're not necessarily here because you want to be and maybe this stuff is boring to you, but is there anything I can help you with in particular, whether it be with injury recovery or in your relationship with God?"

It was at that moment I felt the emotions coming on that I'd been harboring for days, along with the one burning question I had been asking myself: "Mack, if God loves me so much, then why did He allow me to get injured? I had everything going for me and all my hard work was about to pay off. Now I'm probably not getting drafted and my entire baseball career is in jeopardy."

We sat in silence as Mack waited for me to regain composure. "It's a valid question that I've been asked several times," he said calmly. "And my response is always the same. Have you taken the time to go to the Scriptures for yourself to find where it says God had anything to do with your injury?"

For the first time I considered how I'd come to the conclusion that God did this or allowed it to happen. "I guess I've been taught that everything happens for a reason and God's in control. Wouldn't that make my injury part of His plan for my life?"

"Those are more good questions, Jacoby," he said as he stood up to walk around the room. "What you'll quickly learn about me is that I'll always encourage you to go straight to the Scriptures to find out the truth rather than rely on my opinion or the opinions of others. After all, God had His Word written down[6] for our benefit[7] so that we might know Him and all things pertaining to life and godliness.[8] If you'd like, we can go to the Scriptures to see who God's revealed Himself to be and there's a good chance you'll get the answers to those questions."

It dawned on me that I had grown accustomed to believing whatever my reverend and parents taught me without really taking ownership of my relationship with God for myself to see what God says about Himself.

---

[6] **2 Peter 1:20-21 NIV®**: [20]Above all, you must understand that no prophecy of Scripture came about by the prophet's own interpretation of things. [21]For prophecy never had its origin in the human will, but prophets, though human, spoke from God as they were carried along by the Holy Spirit.

[7] **2 Timothy 3:16-17 ESV®**: [16]All Scripture is breathed out by God and profitable for teaching, for reproof, for correction, and for training in righteousness, [17]that the man of God may be complete, equipped for every good work.

[8] **2 Peter 1:3 WT**: His divine power has given us all *things* pertaining to life and godliness through the knowledge [*acknowledgement*] of Him Who called us by His own glory and virtue.

"God's not shy about telling us Who He is," he said pointing to the open Bible in front of me.

"I suppose it couldn't hurt to look," I responded with a glimmer of hope.

"Great. But before we do, I'd like to get an idea of where you feel your relationship with God is at *right now*?"

Who is God and what are some of His characteristics?


Where do your answers to the question above originate?
        (personal study, parents, church, etc.)


Describe your *current* relationship with God.


What's going well in that relationship?


What areas could use improvement?


What do you want to get out of your relationship with God?

How might developing your relationship with God and His Son Jesus Christ impact your life and athletic career?

"I know that God loves me and that He sent His Son to die for my sins so I could live with Him for eternity. But honestly, since my injury I've been angry with God. Everyone keeps telling me He's using this to break me down so He can build me back up, but I don't know – that just never sat right with me and makes me more confused than comforted."

"That's understandable. It doesn't seem like God's nature to be loving and yet allow this to happen," he restated.

"My parents love me and would do anything they could to keep me from harm. I've been taught that God is my Heavenly Father[9] so wouldn't He want the same for me and more? Maybe we *should* go to the Bible to see what God says rather than just go along with what everyone's telling me," I realized.

---

[9] **2 Corinthians 1:3-4 NIV®**: [3]Praise be to the God and Father of our Lord Jesus Christ, the Father of compassion and the God of all comfort, [4]who comforts us in all our troubles, so that we can comfort those in any trouble with the comfort we ourselves receive from God.

24

I could tell Mack was glad I came to that conclusion as he began flipping to the beginning of his Bible. "God doesn't say that you'll never run into trouble in this life but He does say He'll be there to comfort you so you can stay strong during the tough times. You can sit there angry and confused with God and ask, *why me*, or you can take ownership of your situation by going to His Word to get clarity. In sport, the mental game is all about **taking ownership of your thought life to think the best thought possible for the situation, regardless of how you might feel**. Currently, you may *feel* like God had something to do with your injury but let's see what He says about Himself. It doesn't take long for His grand introduction:

Genesis 1:1$^{KJV}$

In the beginning, God created the heaven and the earth.

"Not a bad start to a resume, huh?" Mack joked. "Creator of the heaven and earth."

"I wouldn't mind having that as a conversation starter," I fired back.

"Now let's jump ahead on the Biblical timeline to when the Israelites were slaves in Egypt where God gave Moses instructions to tell them what to call Him:

Exodus 3:13-14<u>NIV®</u>

[13]Moses said to God, "Suppose I go to the Israelites and say to them, 'The God of your fathers has sent me to you,' and they ask me, 'What is his name?' Then what shall I tell them?" [14]God said to Moses, "I *am who* I *am*. This is what you are to say to the Israelites: 'I *am* has sent me to you.'"

"What does *I am who I am* mean?" I asked.

"In Hebrew it means *I will become what I will become*, which was God's way of telling the children of Israel they didn't need to worship any Egyptian gods because He would become whatever they needed Him to become," [10] he explained.

"So God basically said He'd be a one-stop shop for them?" I clarified.

---

[10] [Recorded by B. Chatten] (2004) *God's Law of Prosperity* [CD]. Glen Rock, NJ: Harbor Light Fellowship. CD 2

"That's right. One God for every need. And we see that throughout the Old Testament as He refers to Himself by different titles and promises to be there for His people: like God the Shepherd[11] who takes care of His people, God the Banner (protector)[12], God the Provider[13], the LORD of hosts (armies)[14], the God of peace[15], and one that might be of special interest to you, God the Healer[16], to name a few. We have it even better today in that we get to call God our Heavenly Father since we have His Spirit living within us."[17]

---

[11] **Psalm 23:1 NIV®:** The Lord is my shepherd, I lack nothing.

[12] **Exodus 17:15-16 NIV®:** [15]Moses built an altar and called it The Lord is my Banner. [16]He said, "Because hands were lifted up against the throne of the Lord, the Lord will be at war against the Amalekites from generation to generation."

[13] **Genesis 22:13-14 NIV®:** "[13]Abraham looked up and there in a thicket he saw a ram caught by its horns. He went over and took the ram and sacrificed it as a burnt offering instead of his son. [14]So Abraham called that place The Lord Will Provide. And to this day it is said, "On the mountain of the Lord it will be provided."

[14] **1 Samuel 17:45 KJV:** Then said David to the Philistine, "Thou comest to me with a sword, and with a spear, and with a shield: but I come to thee in the name of the LORD of hosts, the God of the armies of Israel, whom thou hast defied."

[15] **Judges 6:24 NIV®:** So Gideon built an altar to the Lord there and called it The Lord Is Peace. To this day it stands in Ophrah of the Abiezrites.

[16] **Exodus 15:26 NIV®:** He said, "If you listen carefully to the Lord your God and do what is right in his eyes, if you pay attention to his commands and keep all his decrees, I will not bring on you any of the diseases I brought on the Egyptians, for I am the Lord, who heals you."

[17] **Romans 8:14-17 WT:** [14]Accordingly, whoever are led by the spirit that is from God, these are sons of God.) [15]So you have not received a spirit of bondage to again *cause* fear, but you have received a spirit of sonship [*making you sons*], whereby we shout, "Abba," *that is*, "Father." [16]The spirit itself

"That's a lot of names and a lot of abilities," I said. "Can we see what God says about being a God of healing?"

"Sure we can. Remember, the more you know about God, the more confident you'll be in approaching Him in prayer. It takes two to have a relationship and He already knows you better than you know yourself[18] and gave you His Word so that you could know Him well, too. Let's turn to 1 John to learn about God's nature:

1 John 1:5<sup>NIV®</sup>

This is the message we have heard from him and declare to you: God is light; in him there is no darkness at all.

I reread it before saying, "If God is light and there's no darkness in Him at all, then it doesn't seem like His nature to want me injured."

---

bears witness with our own spirit that we are children of God, [17]and since *we are* children, *then we are* heirs also: first of all heirs of God and secondly joint heirs with Christ, so that if we do suffer together, we shall also be glorified together *as heirs*.

[18] **Psalm 139:1-6 NIV®:** [1]You have searched me, Lord, and you know me. [2]You know when I sit and when I rise; you perceive my thoughts from afar. [3]You discern my going out and my lying down; you are familiar with all my ways. [4]Before a word is on my tongue you, Lord, know it completely. [5]You hem me in behind and before, and you lay your hand upon me. [6]Such knowledge is too wonderful for me, too lofty for me to attain.

"Whether you're Christian or not, it's pretty easy to categorize light and darkness; and injuries and setbacks are definitely darkness, which are outside of God's nature to do," he said. "Let's look at Psalms:

Psalm 107:19-21<sup>ESV®</sup>

[19] Then they cried to the Lord in their trouble, and he delivered them from their distress.

[20] He sent out his word and healed them, and delivered them from their destruction.

[21] Let them thank the Lord for his steadfast love, for his wondrous works to the children of man!

"So, God's Word is healing?" I asked.

"That's right. When these people cried out to God, He lovingly sent His Word and it healed them and delivered them from destruction. Let's look at another one in Proverbs:

Proverbs 4:20-22<sup>NIV®</sup>

[20] My son, pay attention to what I say; turn your ear to my words.

[21] Do not let them out of your sight, keep them within your heart;

[22] for they are life to those who find them and health to one's whole body.

"God's Words are life and health to my whole body? That doesn't sound like a God that wants me injured either," I realized.

"And as *you* learn to guard God's Word in your heart and mind, God promises It to be health to your whole body, not just your elbow. But you've got to have the Word in you *first* in order to guard it," he reiterated. "It gets better. God's just as concerned with your heart being healed as He is with your physical body being whole.[19]

"You know, when I walked in here today, I was sure that God had something to do with my injury. And I guess it was based on what I'd heard and been taught, but seeing it with my own eyes that His *very nature* is to heal and wants nothing more than for me to be healed, it makes sense to run towards Him rather than away from Him," I decided. "I know it's up to me to still do my part in physical therapy."

"True. And it's up to us to believe He'll do what He says He'll do, and it's only a choice away. We have the easier part of believing while God has the harder part of bringing His promises to pass. By keeping your eyes fixed on Him and on

---

[19] **Psalm 147:3 NIV®:** He heals the brokenhearted and binds up their wounds.

His ability to heal you, He promises you'll receive the deliverance you need," he encouraged.

"So, I have to ask – if God doesn't want me injured, why did this happen to me?"

"Why *not* you, Jacoby?"

"What do you mean?"

"The simple answer is, injuries happen and every athlete is susceptible to getting hurt, no matter who they are or how great of shape they're in," he said frankly. "Have you considered your arm care routine or your physical preparation?"

He had a point. I figured because I was young I wouldn't get injured, and to go blaming God was just a reaction I had learned at some point that only kept me from taking responsibility for what was in my control in my preparation. I had gotten away from my Jaeger Band arm care exercises when the season started that had been so crucial to my arm health. Maybe I *had* been seeing this all wrong and blaming God for something He hadn't done.

Mack continued, "**The important thing is not wondering *why* it happened to you but *what* you plan to do**

**about it**.  You get to choose how you respond to this injury and that's where having a relationship with God and knowing He wants nothing more than for you to be healed can be the difference maker in your career and life right now in staying strong."

Mack had struck a chord.  A good chord.  Here I was a few days out of surgery and still stuck on the *why me* instead of the *what's next*.  "I hear you, Mack, and now that I know God is for me rather than against me, I feel like it can be a partnership of us going at this together."

Mack nodded his head in agreement.  "There's no profit in feeling sorry for yourself but plenty of profit in believing God's promises while doing your part in physical therapy to the best of your ability.  That's controlling what's in your control and taking a God confidence approach.  Now let's finish up with one more that'll bring this all together:

> 1 John 5:14-15<sup>NIV®</sup>
>
> [14]This is the confidence we have in approaching God:  that if we ask anything according to his will, he hears us.
>
> [15]And if we know that he hears us—whatever we ask—we know that we have what we asked of him.

"Jacoby, the more you know God's Word, the greater confidence you'll have in approaching Him because God's Word is God's will. We just learned His will in regards to healing, which should give you full confidence to approach Him boldly knowing that He hears you and will perform it."

It made perfect sense. How timid would I play if I didn't know the rules of baseball? Why would it be any different in my approach with God if I didn't know His will? "That makes sense. And now I understand why people study the Bible. The more I get to know God, the more trust and confidence I can have in Him to do what He promises to do. I came in today thinking this would be a waste of time but now I'm wondering if it might be exactly what I need right now. Can we meet again next week?"

Mack stood to shake my hand and walked me out. "I have a tight schedule but if you're willing to put in the work, I am willing to make the time. Deal?"

"Deal," I said as he handed me an appointment card.

## Checking for Understanding and for Teaching Others

- Hebrews 11:6$^{WT}$: Now without believing, *it is* impossible to please *God*, for he who approaches God must believe that He is [*exists*] and *that* He becomes a rewarder to those who seek Him. *Know who God is... read His Word... ask with confidence.*
- God's Word is healing to your whole body (Proverbs 4:20-21). Read it and believe it.
- God is light and in Him is no darkness at all (1 John 1:5).
- God is love (1 John 4:8).
- God is faithful (1 Corinthians 1:9).


## Sport Application

- Self-confidence begins in your preparation and is further developed through positive self-talk, positive imagery of seeing yourself succeed in your mind's eye, replaying past successes, seeing your teammates succeed, and displaying huge body language.
- Fear and doubt are the enemies of confidence.
- Confidence requires a moment-by-moment decision to maintain.

What did you learn about who God is in this chapter?


Find 2 verses that support your current needs and take believing action on them:

1.
2.

# Prioritizing Perfect Peace

## Chapter 2

After leaving Mack's office last week I had a new outlook on physical therapy, of me and God going at it together.  However, as the days wore on, thoughts of doubt and fear kept knocking on the door to my heart of whether I'd ever make it back to full strength.  Now, back in Mack's office for a second session, I wanted to learn how to control my thinking when anxious thoughts arise.

"Jacoby, come on in," Mack said, walking out of his office to greet me.

"Thanks for seeing me today," I said as I settled into my chair.

"What were you thinking about in the waiting room when I called you in?  You had a worried look on your face and were about as locked in as a hitter salivating over a 2-0 fastball," he said, noticing my body language.

A little embarrassed that I was showing on the outside what I was feeling on the inside, I responded, "After I left your office last week I was excited to get things going in physical therapy and it was good for a couple days. But when it set in how long I'll be out, it opened the floodgate to all kinds of negative thoughts."

"Negative thoughts like what?"

"Well, I doubt I'll get drafted next month. I'm worried my new college coach will be really upset when I tell him I can't play my freshman year. Everyone's getting better than me right now because I'm stuck in this sling, and to be honest, I'm afraid I might not fully heal from this injury and play competitive baseball ever again," I unloaded in one breath.

"Slow down, Jacoby," he said sympathetically as my eyes began to water. "That sounds like a lot of pressure to take on by yourself. How helpful has it been to dwell on all those doubts, worries, and fears?"

"Not at all. I feel anxious just talking about it. I know I'm supposed to be believing God right now but it's hard when my mind keeps flooding with negatives and I can't seem to stop them. You're the first person I've told," I revealed. "Don't you teach athletes how to control their minds?"

"I appreciate you sharing that with me, and yes, that's a large part of what I do. Would you like to hear my answer from strictly a Sport Psychology perspective or from a Biblical perspective? I can do either or both," Mack posed.

I looked around the room at the numerous examples of success stories before responding, "I guess I'd be curious to hear what you have to say from a Biblical perspective. It seemed to work for all of them."

"What I share with Christian athletes is that from the *world's* perspective, it's normal to have worries, doubts and fears in your situation. And it would be *abnormal* to remain calm and confident in the face of adversity with your athletic career at stake. But God doesn't subscribe to the norms of the world and as His child, neither should you."

"Why not?"

**"Because God desires that we trust Him with all our heart, and as we do so, He promises to direct our paths.[20] With that perspective there's never a situation we need to fear**. If you'd like, I can share some Scriptures that may help

---

[20] **Proverbs 3:5-6 KJV:** [5]Trust in the LORD with all thine heart; and lean not unto thine own understanding. [6]In all thy ways acknowledge him, and he shall direct thy paths.

you see from God's perspective that you don't have to figure everything out on your own," Mack offered.

"I'll give it a try," I said, a bit relieved.

Mack pulled a Bible off the shelf and handed it to me. "If we continue working together, I'll want you to start bringing your own."

"I'll have to find it at home and dust it off," I said half-jokingly.

"Alright, turn to Isaiah 26:3," he said as he leafed through an aged maroon leather Bible with fragile pages sounding as if they'd been turned thousands of times. When he found the verse, he glanced up and saw me looking at it. "A man whose Bible is falling apart is usually a man whose life is not."

I let out a little laugh as I turned to the verse. "That's pretty cheesy but I like it."

"I saw it on a bumper sticker once. Alright, it says:

Isaiah 26:3$^{ESV®}$
You keep him in perfect peace whose mind is stayed on you, because he trusts in you.

"That phrase *perfect peace* in Hebrew means *peace peace,* which is like a double dose of peace," he explained. "As we stay our minds on Him, *who* does the keeping, Jacoby?"

"God does," I answered as I realized I hadn't had any peace in a while, let alone *perfect* peace. "A double dose of peace sounds pretty good about now."

"From what you've shared with me, it sounds like you've got so many things running through your mind that it seems impossible to focus at all. Remember last week when we saw that fear and believing can't exist at the same time? Well, God's Word also says that you can't focus on the things of the world and on God simultaneously; one will always take priority.[21] Would you be willing to try something with me that I think will help you gain some peace?" he asked.

"Sure," I said willing to try anything at this point.

"OK. Read that verse a few times breaking it down into phrases to memorize it."

---

[21] **Matthew 6:24 KJV**: No man can serve two masters: for either he will hate the one, and love the other: or else he will hold to the one, and despise the other. Ye cannot serve God and mammon.

I began muttering the verse to myself, "You keep him in perfect peace... whose mind is stayed on you... because he trusts in you. OK, I think I've got it."

"Now, take a moment to close your eyes and see the verse glide across a huge movie screen one phrase at a time. When you get to the words *perfect peace*, pause, and let them echo in your mind," he instructed.

My curiosity continued to grow as I closed my eyes and quietly began, "You keep him in perfect peace... perfect peace... perfect peace... perfect peace... whose mind is stayed on you... because he trusts in you."

Mack allowed me to go for about a minute before waking me from what seemed like a meditation session. "How was it?"

Smiling, I opened my eyes and admitted, "I feel pretty peaceful right now."

"What were you focusing on?"

"I was focusing on the words *perfect peace* and pausing after *stayed on You*."

"Interesting. Why those phrases?"

"Well, it says God will do the keeping of perfect peace when we stay our minds on Him and trust Him. So I emphasized the source of peace and the outcome of staying my mind on Him."

"And it sounds like you got your desired result?"

Amidst the skepticism I first had, I chose to believe God and had received that peace. "My mind stopped thinking about all the worries, doubts, and fears. I can't tell you the last time I've had any peace."

---

**Your Turn**

Find a quiet place and memorize Isaiah 26:3$^{ESV®}$ by breaking it down into phrases:

"You keep him... in perfect peace... whose mind is stayed on you... because he trusts in you."

Then, take a few minutes and see those words move slowly across your mental movie screen, allowing the phrase "perfect peace" to echo as you believe it. Describe the experience:

---

"I'm glad you were willing to try it out, Jacoby. In Sport Psychology we talk a lot about visualization and positive self-talk but when it comes to God's Word, there's no better food for your mind."

"Why is that?"

"Because God is perfect and so are His Words. So when you choose to make God's Words your words what would that make your self-talk?"

"*Perfect*."

"Bingo. I call it being *God-Inside Minded*. When we choose to make God's thoughts our thoughts, we can be confident they're backed up with power," Mack said, wide-eyed.

"I've heard athletes talk about using positive affirmations like, 'I'm going to get a hit. I'm going to get a hit.' And maybe that works for them but it's never worked for me. I guess it's better than saying, 'I'm going to strike out. I'm going to strike out.' That one seems to work too well," I joked.

Mack laughed a bit in agreement as he leaned in. "Yah, it's definitely better to think positively than negatively in competition but when you elevate your thinking to God's perfect thoughts, it takes self-talk to much higher ground."

"Mack, how did you learn to trust God more?" I asked.

"How does anyone learn to trust someone more?"

"By getting to know them, I suppose."

"Well, your relationship with God works the same way. There's no other way to find out if He's a trustworthy God than to go to His Word and read His track record. I'll save you some time, though. He's never failed a promise but look it up for yourself," he said pointing to the open Bible in my lap.

I flipped through the worn pages, "Like you said last week, God isn't shy about telling us who He is. I just need to read it more."

"I highly recommend it. I also recommend starting off with just a couple of verses and working them in your mind and life until you *know* and *believe* them. It's like making a mechanical adjustment to your swing and practicing it until you're confident enough to transfer it to the game," he said.

"That makes sense. What's the difference between knowing and believing?"

I could tell by the smile on his face that he'd been asked that before. "What's the difference between knowing you have a 90 mph fastball and believing in it?"

Then it clicked. "I guess it's one thing to know I have a 90 mph fastball but it's another to confidently throw it in a 2-0 count with a batter ready to ambush it. If knowing happens in the mind, then believing must be knowledge in action."

"Well said, Jacoby," he confirmed. "It's not enough to know what God's Word says. The benefits come when you take believing action."

"So, in baseball the more I learn to trust my fastball command, the more confidence I'll have to throw it in any count to any batter under any game circumstances. And with God, the more I get to know Him, the more I'll be confident to put my trust in Him in any situation?"

"You've got it."

I reached for the pen and paper I figured was for me. "Do you recommend a starting verse?"

"Why not start with Isaiah 26:3 since you've already memorized it? Write it out and rehearse it throughout the day, and whenever you find your mind beginning to wander towards those worries, doubts, and fears – stop, recognize it, and bring your thinking back to that verse and trust God to re-establish that perfect peace," Mack suggested.

"Sounds simple enough."

"It's simple.  But it won't always be easy.  It will take practice learning to stay your mind on God, just like it takes practice staying your mind in the present moment during competition.

## Checking for Understanding and for Teaching Others

- God promises perfect peace as you stay your mind on Him (Isaiah 26:3).
- God's Words are God-breathed and thus are perfect Words (2 Timothy 3:16).
- Meditating day and night on God's Words helps you think perfect thoughts (Psalm 119:97).
- Believing takes action.  Be a doer of the Word, not just a hearer (James 1:22).

## Sport Application

- Practice staying your mind on what's important *now*.
- Recognize distracting thoughts when they arise and quickly refocus on *now* by using self-talk strategies or repeating a helpful phrase or verse.
- Use visualization to see success before it happens.
- Knowledge minus Believing = Wasted Knowledge.  Take believing action!

Three verses to use as self-talk strategies that will help you become God-inside minded:

1._____

2._____

3._____

Three short performance phrases for between pitches to help you perform in the present moment:

1. _____

2. _____

3. _____

Unless we condition our minds to think the Word, we'll remain at the mercy of the world. **Which one will you choose to become Jacoby – Word conditioned or world conditioned?**"

I'd never thought about that. "I didn't know I had a choice until now. With the little Word conditioning we've done today my heart is feeling lighter and my mindset's feeling stronger already."

"Glad to hear it," Mack said as he stood up to stretch and walk around the room. "The more you practice being God-inside minded, the more your first-thought response will be to remain calm and go to Him. That's how you'll stay cool, calm, and collected under any circumstances."

"That seems like a lot of work to focus on God all the time," I said. "You say it gets easier the more I practice?"

"You won't be able to focus on God *all* the time. I'm just saying not to forget God.[22] With practice, it'll get easier to bring your thinking back to the profitable thoughts of God's Word and harder to get rattled by the world."

"Kind of like on the baseball field when things don't go my way I can get better and better at letting it go and refocusing on the next pitch?" I said in comparison.

"Similar, yes. Whether in sport or in your relationship with God, it's about focusing on the most important thing. God is the most important thing in life and in sport the ball deserves your full attention. I know we touched on a couple already but what were some of those doubts, worries, and fears you're battling right now? I want you to put them down on paper."

Write out your doubts, worries, and fears:

Circle the ones that are completely out of your control and square the ones you can influence.

---

[22] **Psalm 103:2 NIV®:** Praise the LORD, my soul, and forget not all his benefits—

I grabbed the pen and paper and began pouring out: "Mainly my feelings and emotions about the injury have got me pretty down. Then I start thinking about the draft next month and whether my surgery went well and if I'll ever recover to full strength. I think about the expectations I have for myself and from others who've put so much time and effort into helping me succeed. I don't want to let anyone down."

"Understandable. You've worked hard to get where you're at and a lot of people have had a hand in that," Mack sympathized. "Do you do that on the mound, too? I mean, do you do a lot of thinking out there?"

My last few outings had been pretty bad but I never evaluated what might've been the cause. Thinking too much was likely it. How could I expect to be successful with a mind preoccupied with mechanics, expectations, listening to coaches, being quick to home with runners on, the past, and the future? I was no longer keeping it simple by trusting my stuff and competing with what I had. "That was probably my downfall towards the end. I was thinking about everything except the pitch I was throwing."

"Isn't it interesting in Isaiah 26:3 that God gives us *one thing* to focus on?  Him," Mack pointed out.  "There may be something to that in other areas of life, too.  God designed the mind and knows how it functions best.  In life, it all starts with remembering God's goodness and faithfulness to His Word and bringing your mind back to Him when it starts to wander.  That's when we start seeing His ability bigger than our problems," Mack reminded me.  "In sport, when your mind starts running towards negative town, establishing routines to bring you back to the present moment will be the difference maker.  From what you wrote down, what did you notice you tend to focus on?"

I picked up the paper and saw a lot of circled words.  "I've been focusing on things that I can't even do anything about.  But my mind seems to go there so quickly that it's hard to keep those negative thoughts from pushing their way in," I said honestly.

"Here's a silly example but it may help.  When a puppy is in training, does it automatically stay the first time its owner gives the command?"

"No."

"Well, think of your mind as a puppy in training. If you leave it by itself, it's going to tear everything up. But with training, it will learn to stay still. For a puppy, staying put for five seconds feels like an eternity. Then it learns to stay for ten seconds, then twenty. Eventually, the owner can leave the room and the puppy will stay put. Your mind works similarly and as you learn to take care of your thoughts, they'll take care of you. It takes practice and training. But it's achievable."

I felt like that puppy making a mess. "I think I'll start with just one minute of staying my mind on Isaiah 26:3 every day," I decided.

Mack gave a look of approval. "That's how it starts. Now let's look at what God says about worrying.

> Matthew 6:25-27<sup>NKJV®</sup>
> **25** "Therefore I say to you, do not worry about your life, what you will eat or what you will drink; nor about your body, what you will put on. Is not life more than food and the body more than clothing?
> **26** Look at the birds of the air, for they neither sow nor reap nor gather into barns; yet your heavenly Father feeds them. Are you not of more value than they?

**²⁷** Which of you by worrying can add one cubit to his stature?

"Jacoby, if God takes care of the birds, don't you think He has you covered?  That word *worry* means to be mentally distracted, overly concerned or anxious with too much care. What does God tell us to do when it comes to worrying?" Mack asked.

"He tells us *not* to do it."

"And how much good does God say worrying does exactly?"

I began to laugh as I could tell Mack was driving home God's point.  "He says worrying does about as much good as trying to grow taller by worrying!"

"Go ahead and try it, Jacoby.  Worry yourself into being taller.  Worry your elbow into being healed.  Worry yourself into next month's draft," Mack playfully demanded.

How much time had I spent worrying about my future, my injury, my baseball career, and life?  "I get it.  God's saying it's as pointless to worry as it is to try and force myself to grow."

"Sounds kind of funny when you say it out loud, doesn't it?  Let's keep reading:

Matthew 6:28-34[NKJV®]

[28]"So why do you worry about clothing?  Consider the lilies of the field, how they grow:  they neither toil nor spin;

[29]and yet I say to you that even Solomon in all his glory was not arrayed like one of these.

[30]Now if God so clothes the grass of the field, which today is, and tomorrow is thrown into the oven, *will He* not much more *clothe* you, O you of little faith?

[31]"Therefore do not worry, saying, 'What shall we eat?' or 'What shall we drink?' or 'What shall we wear?'

[32]For after all these things the Gentiles seek.  For your heavenly Father knows that you need all these things.

[33]But seek first the kingdom of God and His righteousness, and all these things shall be added to you.

$^{34}$Therefore do not worry about tomorrow, for tomorrow will worry about its own things. Sufficient for the day *is* its own trouble."

"God's solution to anxiety is to seek Him *first* and He'll meet our needs," Mack reiterated. "Are you getting the point that God doesn't want you anxious at all?"

It was becoming clear how worry-proof seeking God first could be. Heck, if He takes care of the flowers and grass, wouldn't He make sure I was taken care of, too? "If God's saying not to be anxious even a little bit, it must be possible. Who are the Gentiles?"

"In the Bible, Gentiles are often referred to as people not of a Judean background or people who didn't believe in God. God explains how unbelievers spend their lives full of anxiety and stressed trying to figure out how they'll get their needs met on their own. We're instructed to *not* be like them," he emphasized before taking a sip of water. "Our job is to seek God first in prayer and He will meet our every need. In baseball, your job as a pitcher is to focus on hitting the glove and thinking the best thought possible for the situation despite the circumstances. Did you catch in verse 30 what was called into question?"

"Their believing.  Similar to how Jesus asked Peter on the water."

"Exactly.  This group of people was being reminded to get back to believing God rather than allowing anxious thoughts to steal their focus so easily," he explained.

I was amazed at how what we consider to be the most important essentials in life God just calls *things*.  "I liked in verse 25 where it says, 'Isn't life more than food and the body more than clothing?'  It sounds like God's saying there's more to life than worrying about how we're going to make it through the day."

"That's exactly what He's saying and there *is* more to life, Jacoby.  Everyone has needs but we get to choose whether we get all anxious about them or get excited to look to God as our provider and watch as He supplies in ways only He can," Mack concluded.

This was way different from the path my mind naturally went but it was helping me see how much bigger God was than my problems.

## Checking for Understanding and for Teaching Others

- God's solution to anxiety is to seek Him first.
- The excitement of this life is not in getting *things* but in confidently expecting God to provide in ways that only He can and thanking Him when He answers prayers.
- Today is all you need to invest your focus on. You don't know what tomorrow holds but you know Who holds tomorrow.

### Sport Application

- Focus on one pitch at a time... not the past, not the future.
- Know the best thing to think in each situation. Then act on it confidently.
- Allow yourself to compete free of distractions by learning to focus your attention on what's inside your influence rather than on the many things outside your control.

**Name 4 things in your control that would improve your performance if you gave them your focus rather than allow your focus to be stolen by things outside your control.**

**1.**

**2.**

**3.**

**4.**

"Do you remember in school when you were first learning how to simplify fractions?" Mack asked as he handed me a math problem. "For instance, simplify two over four?"

"Easy. One half."

Mack retrieved the paper and took a bit longer to write the next one: "Now, simplify 1,000,000/2,000,000."

It took me a second to filter all the zeros before realizing it was the same, "One half, again."

"At first glance it can be intimidating to see that huge fraction but when you break it down to its simplest form, it's not complicated at all. Think about all the *zeros* in baseball like the fans, score, stats, money, expectations, and so on. They can all distract you from keeping the game really simple between a batter, a ball, and a pitcher," Mack said.

I got up and circled the room as I considered all the fluff I was allowing to complicate the game from its simplicity of one pitcher, one batter, and one pitch at a time. Simple is always better. **I just needed to do simple *better*.** "God is asking me to simplify life too, isn't He? Don't get anxious. Instead, seek Him first."

"Yes. And now you have the awareness to help you to stop and recognize what you're focusing on at any given time and refocus on what's most important," Mack added.

"That's a good idea. Hey, I was noticing that last verse about not worrying about tomorrow. I'm realizing I often worry so much about the future that I don't live or play in the present moment."

"I'm glad you saw that. Anxiety lives in the future. In the unknown. But God says not to worry about the future because there's enough going on today to devote our attention. Plus, in seeking God first, we know that He'll provide for us tomorrow just like He promises to do today," he reminded me.

"It sounds like a lifetime effort."

"One well worth the effort.

"Would you say a good way to seek God first is to go to Him in prayer?" I asked.

"It's a great way because God is always accessible. We really have the easy job of praying and we need to let Him do the part He delights in, which is answering our prayers.[23] The part, we need to realize, we can't do."

"That's kind of embarrassing to think that we would try to do God's job," I said. "But I guess we try to do it all the time and just end up stressed out."

---

[23] **Proverbs 15:8 KJV**: The sacrifice of the wicked is an abomination to the LORD: but the prayer of the upright is his delight.

"Well, we can't do His job any more than He can do ours. I'm often guilty of it myself. God asks us to bring our requests to Him and seek Him first above any other source," he said.

## Checking for Understanding and for Teaching Others

- The bigger we see God, the smaller we'll see life's problems.
- Your prayer life is a great way to check in with God and get peaceful.
- **Visualization Practice:** See yourself encountering life's obstacles and pausing to check in with God. See yourself smiling, staying calm and doing your part while waiting in confident expectation for God to do His.
- Do this... a lot. It will become your first-thought response.

## Sport Application

- Become aware of the distractions that keep you from checking in with yourself each pitch and work to eliminate them by practicing your between-pitch routines in your room using visualization. See yourself running through your routines flawlessly and bypassing those distractions that tend to trip you up.
- Do this... a lot. It will become your first-thought response.

"Jacoby, something you said earlier sparked a few verses that I'd like to share with you before we close out today's session," Mack remembered. "You mentioned your emotions and feelings sometimes get you down. I want to share with you God's thoughts on negative emotions like anxiety and what we should do with them:

Philippians 4:6-7[WT]
6Do not be anxious [*distracted*] about anything, but in everything, by prayer and prayer request with thanksgiving, let your petitions be made known to God,

7and the peace of God, which is more excellent than every way of thinking, will protect your hearts and your thinking in Christ Jesus.

"Do not be anxious," I whispered as I reread the passage with my face closer to the pages, "...about anything, but in everything, by prayer, with thanksgiving, let your petitions be made known unto God, and the peace of God, which is more excellent than every way of thinking, will protect your hearts and your thinking in Christ Jesus. It says don't be anxious about *anything*."

"God wouldn't ask us to do something we're incapable of doing. So if God tells us *not* to be anxious about anything –"

"Then it's possible to be free of anxiety *and* have the peace of God no matter what's going on," I interrupted.

"God wouldn't have us to be anxious at all. When you begin to grasp the magnitude of this, the only thing you'll be left asking yourself is what you'll do with all that extra time you're no longer wasting on worrying!" Mack said.

What a true statement. I could use that newfound time to work on my mental game by visualizing myself on the mound throwing to batters and controlling my mind to think the best thoughts possible while simulating the ups and downs an inning can bring.

Mack continued, "When you find yourself beginning to dwell on the future, be anxious for nothing and pray instead. When your mind starts to worry about the draft, be anxious for nothing and pray instead. When you start worrying about all the guys getting better this summer while you're recovering, be anxious for nothing and pray instead. When you start to doubt your ability to pitch like before, be anxious for nothing and pray instead. When you wonder if your new coach will be disappointed with you, be anxious for nothing and pray instead. When you find yourself worrying if you'll ever realize your Major League dream, be anxious for nothing and pray instead."

I began grasping how worry-proof God designed the mind to be and the strategy for staying peaceful. No matter the circumstances it was possible to have perfect peace and maintain a cool, calm, and collected approach.

"There'll be plenty of positive and negative thoughts on your journey ahead but now you've got the choice of which ones you'll entertain and retain. Remember, there's absolutely no profit to worrying but plenty of profit in having a peaceful heart and mind on and off the field. While the rest of the world stays busy worrying, you get busy trusting God. You'll see the fruit of that decision immediately," Mack said confidently.

"I think my biggest takeaway today has been learning that peace is not random. It's always in relation to me controlling and directing my thinking to what's most important."

"That's a solid takeaway. Now go put it into action. I know we went a little long today but I hope our time together has been helpful. You coming in for sessions is a testament to you doing everything in your control to getting back to playing ball," Mack commended.

"This stuff's great. I'm feeling a lot better already. Thanks again, Mack, for your time."

He handed me another appointment card as he walked me out. Before driving away I flipped over the card where 1 Peter 5:7[NIV®] was printed: "Cast all your anxiety on him because he cares for you." How timely. Driving away I felt proud to be Christian for the first time in a while. How could I have done this any other way?

## Checking for Understanding and for Teaching Others

- God says to be anxious for *nothing*! Instead, in *everything* by prayer bring your requests to Him and He promises a peace more excellent than any way of thinking (Philippians 4:6-7).
- Be God's Word Conditioned rather than world conditioned.

## Sport Application

- Allow your actions to be driven by right thinking rather than emotional sinking.
- Take care of your thought life and it will take care of you.
- Become unshakeable in your thought life by spending your mental energy on things in your control that matter *now*.
- Action happens in the present. Be there for it. Let others dwell on the past or worry about the future. Competitive advantage... you.

# The Purpose-Full Mission

## Chapter 3

Another week of physical therapy had passed with what felt like slow progress. Keeping Isaiah 26:3 in mind was helping to banish the negative thoughts but as it continued to set in how long I'd be without baseball, I couldn't help but grow a little aimless. Walking into Mack's office, I was hoping for some direction.

"Jacoby, come on in," Mack said with a huge smile on his face as he hung up the phone. "How are you?"

"I'm alright. Feeling like I need some direction," I answered. "It's starting to hit me again how long the road to recovery will be."

Mack looked at me with empathy. "That's understandable. Physical therapy can be a grind when the end goal seems so far away."

"Have any of your other clients gone through injuries like this?" I asked.

"Several. Actually, I just got off the phone with a former client who also had Tommy John surgery a few years back and was calling to let me know he's making his Major League debut this weekend. I'm flying out to watch."

"Congrats, Mack. That's got to be exciting," I said, feeling somewhat encouraged about my situation. "What did you guys work on together when he was recovering?"

"He called to thank me for a particular conversation we had about developing and clarifying his mission. He said it was a game changer for him in dominating rehab to get back to pursuing his Major League dream," Mack stated.

"Sounds like it worked for him," I said wondering if I'd ever established my mission. "Can we have a similar conversation?"

"Sure we can. I can't promise you the same results he earned but if you develop a mission that's *purpose-full,* it'll give you the direction to persevere throughout your career. Let's start by answering a few questions. Why do you want to play professional baseball?"

I immediately lit up and smiled ear to ear as I thought of all the reasons I wanted to suit up for a Major League team. "I love baseball. It's all I've ever wanted to do. The big games, the lifestyle, the money, the girls, the travel, the perks, and fans wanting my autograph are all I think about."

I could tell Mack had heard it all before. "Those are some good motivators but what will keep you going once you've made it to the Majors and have all that?"

I couldn't imagine ever getting bored of those things. "Then I'll want to make the Hall of Fame."

"OK. Let's say you're at your Hall of Fame acceptance dinner and your former teammates are cracking a few jokes before settling in to share about the kind of man you were on and off the field, how you impacted them, and how you influenced the game. What would you want them to say?"

I'd never thought to **begin with the end goal in mind**. "I definitely want to be remembered as a bulldog on the mound who never backed down and a clutch player who loved to perform on the biggest stages. And, of course, I want people to say I was a good teammate and hard worker."

"How about off the field?"

"I guess if we're talking about the end of my career, I'd like people to say I was generous with my time and signed a lot of autographs. That I was a role model for young athletes and a good husband and father even with the demands of a baseball schedule."

"Those are all good things," Mack said. "So when do you plan to start earning that reputation?"

I then understood why he was asking me about the Hall of Fame dinner. "**If I want to be remembered for those things at the end of my career, I have to start doing them _today_.**"

"There you go. I've found in working with athletes that the clearer they are on what _mission accomplished_ looks like, the less they're willing to budge or make excuses when things get hard," he shared. "Now, how valuable is your baseball career to you?"

That one was easy. "It's pretty much the most important thing in my life."

"If that's the case, what are you willing to sacrifice to attain your dream of playing pro ball? **Everyone wants to get there but few are willing to do what it takes. If you want**

**what few people ever get, you've got to do what few people are willing to do**."

I felt like I'd already given up a lot but I understood what he was getting at. "I'll need to go to bed earlier to be fresh for early morning workouts. I'll have to get to practice earlier and stay later than anyone. I might have to hold off on relationships for a while to focus on school and baseball, and I know I'll miss out on a lot of fun kids my age are having."

"Will you be willing to give those up on a consistent basis? Demands on your time are only going to increase as your baseball stock rises. I'm not trying to discourage you; I just want you as prepared as possible for the road ahead."

I appreciated what he was saying. "I've thought a lot about it and all I've ever wanted to do is play pro ball. I know it won't be easy but I really want it."

Mack sensed my enthusiasm but from years of experience he knew all too well enthusiasm wouldn't be enough for the grind awaiting me. "Wanting to play professional baseball just to say you made it and to enjoy the lifestyle won't be enough. That's why you've got to make your mission *purpose-full*."

"What do you mean?" I asked. "Like, full of purpose?"

"Yes. It's clear your mission is to play at the highest level but for what *purpose*? To say you made it? Jacoby, you'll have the opportunity to influence a lot of people along the way and more when you arrive. Most athletes are so concerned with just getting there that they never consider the kind of impact they want to make on the audience they're given."

I got up and walked around the office looking at the pictures of accomplished athletes lining the walls. I had heard of guys making it to the top only to experience an empty feeling after the excitement of riches and fame wore off. "I see what you're saying and to be honest, I don't know that I have an answer for you right now. At this point I *am* just trying to get there. What was the *purpose-full* mission you and that client decided on a few years back that just earned him a plane ticket to the Big Leagues?"

"At the time he was feeling a bit aimless too so we looked at the greatest example ever of a man on a mission to see if he could gain some inspiration and direction to become a man on a Big League mission."

"Who was the man and what was his mission?" I asked with deepening curiosity.

"Jesus." Mack told me. "His mission from God was to be the Savior of the world *so that* anyone who believes on his name becomes born of God's Spirit and receives the promise of eternal life.[24] **Once my client learned of all that God by way of His Son Jesus Christ had done for him, he made it his mission to reach the Major Leagues with the purpose of sharing God's Word with the world**. It wasn't about the money, the women, the fame or the stats anymore. His real joy came from having the opportunity to play the game he loved and have an audience to share how good God and Jesus Christ are. The rest was just a bonus. *That's* what I mean by making your mission *purpose-full*."

It all began to make sense. The photos of Christian athletes I'd been staring at for three sessions had reached the pinnacle of their sport and credited their relationship with God for being a major contributing factor. "There had to be something to it," I thought to myself.

---

[24] **1 John 4:14-15 WT:** [14]and we have seen and we are bearing witness that the Father has sent the Son *to be* the savior of the world. [15]Whoever confesses that Jesus is the Son of God, God abides in him and he in God,

"If you'd like, we can look at the *purpose* behind God sending Jesus Christ to save the world in a little more depth to see if it does for you what it did for my client," Mack proposed.

"I think I should at least hear you out. It seemed to work for him and all of them," I told him as I acknowledged the pictures before sitting back down.

Mack reached for a couple Bibles on the shelf and handed me one, noticing I hadn't brought mine. "Has anyone ever asked you if you've accepted Jesus as your lord and Savior?"[25]

"Of course. That's how I became Christian."

"And have you ever wondered *why* you needed saving?"

I knew I was saved from my sins[26] but besides that I hadn't really thought about it. "I guess I've never asked. Why *did* I need saving?"

---

[25] **Romans 10:9-10 NIV®**: [9]If you declare with your mouth, "Jesus is Lord," and believe in your heart that God raised him from the dead, you will be saved. [10]For it is with your heart that you believe and are justified, and it is with your mouth that you profess your faith and are saved.

[26] **1 John 4:9-10 NIV®**: [9]This is how God showed his love among us: He sent his one and only Son into the world that we might live through him. [10]This is love: not that we loved God, but that he loved us and sent his Son as an atoning sacrifice for our sins.

"Let's go to the Scriptures to see what *they* say. They'll do a much better job of explaining it than I ever could. In looking at this you'll understand why you needed saving and the role Jesus Christ played as your Savior. It'll be important to know this stuff if you ever decide to make sharing God's Word with the world your *purpose-full* mission. Let's start in Genesis chapter one:

> Genesis 1:31$^{KJV}$
>
> And God saw every thing that he had made, and, behold, it was very good. And the evening and the morning were the sixth day.

"If everything was *very* good, why did we need saving?" I asked, potentially jumping the gun.

Mack could tell my interest was growing. "Let's look a few verses back at one of the things God had made that He said was *very* good and see if it stayed that way:

> Genesis 1:26-27$^{ESV®}$
>
> $^{26}$Then God said, "Let us make man in our image, after our likeness. And let them have dominion over the fish of the sea and over the birds of the heavens and over the livestock and over all the

earth and over every creeping thing that creeps on the earth."

<sup>27</sup>So God created man in his own image, in the image of God he created him; male and female he created them.

"What's God's image?" I asked.

"In the Gospel of John it says that God's image is spirit."[27]

"So if God is spirit, then God created man to have spirit?"

"That's right.  And the first man was Adam.  Keep in mind, we're still trying to figure out *why* the world needed saving.  Let's look at what else Adam was made with back in Genesis:

Genesis 2:7<sup>KJV</sup>

And the Lord God formed man *of* the dust of the ground, and breathed into his nostrils the breath of life; and man became a living soul.

---

<sup>27</sup> **John 4:24 ESV®**: "God is spirit, and those who worship him must worship in spirit and truth."

"So, it looks like God originally created Adam in His image which is **spirit**, then formed a **body** for him from the dust of the ground and breathed **soul** life into him, making him a three-part being of body, soul, and spirit?" I confirmed.

"Correct. Originally, there were two types of life in Adam's body. **Spirit life, which gave man the ability to relate to God**[28] **and soul life that allowed Adam to live and breathe and relate to the world**. It's interesting to note that God created man with spirit life *before* making him a body and breathing into him soul life. Makes you wonder how important God considered having a spiritual connection with man, doesn't it?"

I had never understood the difference between spirit and soul life until then and I could see the plot developing of what might've happened that caused a need for a Savior. "I'm guessing something happened to Adam's spirit life to where things were no longer *very* good and I bet that's where man's need for a Savior comes into play."

"You got it. Adam, who God had made a complete being of body, soul, and spirit, and in perfect communication

---

[28] **Romans 8:9 WT**: You are not in the flesh but in the spirit, since the spirit from God dwells in you. If anyone does not have the spirit, that is to say, Christ, *then* he does not belong to him,

with Him, was given one rule to follow; and if he chose to break that rule, God promised him that the consequences for disobeying would be certain death."[29]

"He broke that one rule, didn't he?" I predicted.

"Yes. And he certainly died that day."

"But didn't Adam have kids and live a long time *after* that?"

"He did and lived to be 930 years old.[30] So, if Adam's soul life didn't die that day, what life form in him must have died?" Mack asked.

"*Spirit* life," I answered as it began to make more sense. "Does that mean he also lost the ability to communicate with God?"

"He sure did. God can only communicate with what He is so when spirit life in man died – so did God's ability to communicate with man."

---

[29] **Genesis 2:16-17 NIV®:** And the Lord God commanded the man, "You are free to eat from any tree in the garden; but you must not eat from the tree of the knowledge of good and evil, for when you eat from it you will certainly die."

[30] **Genesis 5:5 NIV®:** Altogether, Adam lived a total of 930 years, and then he died.

"And Adam's disobedience caused that," I interjected.

"And those weren't the only changes that occurred as a result of Adam's sin. Before that, there was no mention of death, sickness, injuries, fear or pain but we read about all those things throughout the Bible from then on. To make things worse, not only did Adam lose spirit life for himself but also for everyone after him, who've all been born in his *new* image of only body and soul and separated from God[31] even though they hadn't sinned the way he did."[32]

"So God never intended for people to die or suffer pain?"

"Never. Some people call death a friend but God calls death the last enemy to be defeated.[33]

---

[31] **Genesis 5:3 NIV®:** When Adam had lived 130 years, he had a son in his own likeness, in his own image; and he named him Seth.

[32] **Romans 5:12 & 14 WT:** [12]Therefore, as by one man the sin entered into the world and the death by the sin, even so the death passed unto all men, by which all have sinned. [14]Nevertheless, the death *still* reigned from Adam until Moses, even over them who had not sinned after the likeness of Adam's transgression, who is a type of him who was to come.

[33] **1 Corinthians 15:26 KJV:** The last enemy *that* shall be defeated *is* death.

## Checking for Understanding and for Teaching Others

- God originally designed man completely perfect and to live with Him forever in paradise.

- Adam's willful disobedience caused man to lose:
  - Spirit life and thus the ability to have a relationship with God.
  - Eternal life with God, which was His original design.

- Changes to what was *very good* as a consequence of Adam's disobedience:
  - Sin entered (Romans 5:12).
  - Death entered (Romans 5:12).

- The state of man and the world:
  - In need of a saving by way of a Savior

I felt like I needed a breather after all that. "Adam really left us in a bad place with one poor decision, didn't he?"

"He sure did and in need of major saving. But right after he blew the *perfect* game by disobeying God and eating of the fruit he was told not to eat[34] God took immediate

---

[34] **Genesis 3:11-14 NIV®**: [11]And he said, "Who told you that you were naked? Have you eaten from the tree that I commanded you not to eat from?" [12]The man said, "The woman you put here with me—she gave me some fruit from the tree, and I ate it." [13]Then the Lord God said to the woman, "What is this you have done?" The woman said, "The serpent deceived me, and I ate." [14]So the Lord God said to the serpent, "Because you have done this, Cursed are you above all livestock and all wild animals! You will crawl on your belly and you will eat dust all the days of your life."

action by declaring a plan to repair the spirit relationship between Him and mankind."

"And that plan involved a Savior to rescue man from *spiritual* death?"

"Yes, I can tell you're paying attention!  Let's read in Genesis 3:15 God's declaration to the serpent about His plan of salvation:

> Genesis 3:15 $^{NIV®}$
>
> And I will put enmity between you and the woman, and between your offspring and hers; he will crush your head, and you will strike his heel."

"I'm not sure I get what that all means," I said.

"This is God's declaration to the devil that He would one day send a Savior born of a woman to utterly destroy him for being the root cause of man's ruined relationship with God but that the devil would briefly injure the Savior.  We see that come to fruition when the devil had Jesus Christ crucified, but then God raised him from the dead and has sat him at His right hand in heaven until all his enemies are to be made his footstool."[35]

I was in awe of the precision with which God had laid out His plan way back in Genesis and how Jesus Christ carried it out perfectly to repair man's relationship with God thousands of years later. What a God and what a Savior in Jesus Christ!

Mack continued, "Jesus Christ conquered death just like God declared he would[36] but for now the devil is still around doing evil and so is physical death. But when God sends Jesus Christ back for us, the devil will be utterly destroyed[37] and so will death.[38] God sure didn't waste any time in declaring His mission for a Savior to rescue mankind, huh?" Mack finished.

---

[35] **Hebrews 10:12-13 ESV®**: [12]But when Christ had offered for all time a single sacrifice for sins, he sat down at the right hand of God, [13]waiting from that time until his enemies should be made a footstool for his feet.

[36] **Romans 6:9 KJV**: Knowing that Christ being raised from the dead dieth no more; death hath no more dominion over him.

[37] **Revelation 20:10 KJV**: And the devil that deceived them was cast into the lake of fire and brimstone, where the beast and the false prophet *are*, and shall be tormented day and night for ever and ever.

[38] **Revelation 21:4 KJV**: And God shall wipe away all tears from their eyes; and there shall be no more death, neither sorrow, nor crying, neither shall there be any more pain: for the former things are passed away.

"I guess having a relationship with us meant that much to Him," I responded. "So God was the Author of the plan of salvation and Jesus Christ was the Savior that carried it out?"

"That's right, you're learning quick. That's why God is credited in some Scriptures with being our Savior [39] even though it was Jesus that performed the mission."

"So, would God's declaration in Genesis 3:15 basically be Him starting with the end goal in mind to one day have a relationship with man again?"

"He certainly had that end goal in mind and we can see the outcome of Jesus Christ's mission on earth in Acts chapter 1 in his last words to his disciples just before his ascension:

> Acts 1:4-5<sup>WT</sup> & 8-9<sup>WT</sup>
>
> [4]So, being salted together *with them*, he charged them to not depart from Jerusalem but to wait for the promise [*what was promised*] of the Father, 'which,' *he said*, 'you heard of me,

---

[39] **Jude 1:24-25 KJV**: [24]Now unto him that is able to keep you from falling, and to present *you* faultless before the presence of his glory with exceeding joy, [25]To the only wise God our Savior, *be* glory and majesty, dominion and power, both now and ever. Amen.

<sup>5</sup>"that John indeed baptized with water but you will be baptized with holy spirit not many days from now.'

<sup>8'</sup>However, you will receive power when the holy spirit comes upon you, and you will be my witnesses not only in Jerusalem but also in all Judea and Samaria and to the farthest *part* of the earth.'

<sup>9</sup>Having said these *things*, he was lifted up, and a cloud received him out of their sight as they watched."

I hadn't ever read Jesus' last words on earth before. "I bet God was eager to have a relationship with man again after waiting for so long."

"Well, He didn't wait long to make the gift of holy spirit available for all men, which you can read about in Acts chapter two, where ten days after Jesus' ascension on the day of Pentecost[40] holy spirit was poured out on the 12 apostles and

---

[40] **Acts 2:1-4 WT**: <sup>1</sup>Now when the Day of Pentecost had fully come, they [*the twelve apostles*] were all together with unity of purpose. <sup>2</sup>Then suddenly a sound from heaven as of a rushing, forceful breath came and filled the whole house where they were sitting, <sup>3</sup>and there appeared tongues as of fire, which were distributed to them, and it sat upon each one of them. <sup>4</sup>Then they were

then about 3,000 people got saved the same day![41] That was the birthday of Christianity and the rebirth of God and man's ability to communicate!"

I felt like we had just summed up the Bible in a matter of minutes. What Adam messed up Jesus Christ fully repaired. Incredible. "Mack, why is it called *the gift* of holy spirit?"

"Because God made holy spirit available for *free* as a gift to mankind. What cost God the life of His dear Son only cost us one moment of genuine humility in confessing Jesus as lord and believing that God raised him from the dead.[42] We didn't do anything to earn it[43] and this time we can't lose it."[44]

---

all filled with holy spirit, and they began to speak in other tongues, as the Spirit was giving them [*the words*] to speak out.

[41] **Acts 2:38-40 WT:** [38]Peter said to them: "Repent and be baptized in the name of Jesus Christ, every one of you, for the forgiveness of your sins, and you will receive the gift from the Holy Spirit. [39]"Certainly, the promise is for you and for your children and for all who are far off, whomever our Lord God will call to Himself." [40]With many other words, he testified and exhorted them, saying, "Be saved [*delivered*] from this crooked generation." [41]So then, those who accepted his word were baptized [*in the name of Jesus Christ*], and there were added *to them* in that day about 3000 souls.

[42] **Ephesians 1:13 WT:** In him [*the Christ*] you also, after you heard the word of the truth, the gospel of your salvation [*deliverance*], having also believed in him, were sealed with the holy spirit of promise,

[43] **Ephesians 2:8-9 WT:** [8]By grace, you have certainly been saved [*delivered*] through believing, and this [*salvation*] *is* not from yourselves. *It is* the offering of God. [9]*It is* not of *our* works so that no one may boast,

[44] **1 Peter 1:23 KJV:** Being born again, not of corruptible seed, but of incorruptible, by the word of God, which liveth and abideth for ever.

I was completely humbled as I tried to grasp the enormity of all that God and Jesus Christ had done for me. "How could *one moment* of humility get me an *eternity* with them? I feel like we have to do so little."

"**Because it cost God and Jesus Christ so much**. God wouldn't have put His Son through all that just to make salvation really difficult to attain. Remember, all God has ever wanted is a relationship again with man so He made it as easy as possible to receive spirit life."

I had to laugh inside as only God in His infinite wisdom could come up with that kind of plan. "It should've been us reaching out to God, yet He chose to reach out to us?[45] I just lost any reason I might've had to be boastful in life about anything other than God and Jesus Christ."

"I agree. In sport, you earn everything you get and should take credit for it, but with God we didn't earn or deserve anything and He gave us everything."[46]

---

[45] **1 John 4:10 NIV®:** This is love: not that we loved God, but that he loved us and sent his Son as an atoning sacrifice for our sins.

[46] **Titus 3:4-7 WT:** [4]However, when the kindness and friendliness of God, our Savior, appeared, [5]not by works of justice that we did but according to His mercy, He saved [*delivered*] us through the washing of being born again and the renewing of holy spirit, [6]which He poured out upon us richly through Jesus Christ, our Savior, [7]so that having been justified by that grace, we became heirs according to the hope of eternal life.

It was all so much to digest but seeing it clearly from the Scriptures made it easier to understand. "It helps to see the **big-picture mission** of man's need for a Savior to understand the ***purpose*** for Jesus Christ accomplishing that mission. I need to use the bathroom but when I get back, I'd like to see *how* Jesus did it all."

"Sounds good. I know it took a bit longer than expected but if you decide to make God's mission your mission in speaking God's Word to the world like Jesus instructed his disciples to do right before he ascended, it'll be good to know from the Scriptures why people need saving. We've got greater access now to God than at any other time in history since Adam."

## Checking for Understanding and for Teaching Others

- God saw the *new* state of man of just body and soul and disconnected from Him and declared a plan to send a Savior to repair the spiritual relationship that Adam had lost.

- God determined that if one man (Adam) by free will messed everything up, one man born of a woman would later by the freedom of his will be a perfect sacrifice to repair everything (1 Corinthians 15:20-23).

- Everything Adam *had* lost, Jesus Christ *has* fully recovered to never be lost again!

## Sport Application

- Once you've determined your mission, *declare it*.

- Make it *purpose-full*.

- Understand the timeline and need for patience.

- Understand the potential sacrifices.

- Start with the end goal in mind and align all your actions with it.

- Start your mission. Stick to your mission. Complete your mission.

**When you ask others if they've accepted Jesus as their lord and Savior and they ask you why they need saving, how will you respond? Write down the Scriptures you'll use and share with others:**

What three parts did God originally make man?

What part was lost due to Adam's sin?

Where did that leave man in relation to God?

What did God immediately declare in Genesis 3:15 that He would do?

What must any man believe in order to be saved?
(Romans 10:9-10)

# Mission Possible Perspective

## Chapter 4

Walking back from the bathroom I considered what Mack had said about potentially making my *purpose-full* mission one for God's glory.  As I sat back down, he was already looking up our starting point for *how* Jesus accomplished his mission.

He started in, "The Scriptures don't say *exactly* when Jesus would've known and understood what he was to do, but They do indicate that by age twelve he was already about his Father's business[47] and in the Temple learning from the top Judean teachers."[48]

---

[47] **Luke 2:49 NKJV®:**  And He said to them, "Why did you seek Me?  Did you not know that I must be about My Father's business?"

[48] **Luke 2:46-47 NIV®:**  [46]After three days they found him in the temple courts, sitting among the teachers, listening to them and asking them questions.  [47]Everyone who heard him was amazed at his understanding and his answers.

"At *twelve?*" I said in amazement. "Talk about all-out dedication. I've wanted to play baseball since I was a kid but that's a little different than taking on the responsibility of saving the world. Did he know what he'd have to endure at that age?"

"It doesn't say but he definitely would have prepared himself for what was to come by reading the book of Isaiah. Jacoby, **before committing to a mission it's crucial that you understand what lies ahead. The better prepared you are, the greater your ability to handle the adversity awaiting you**," he told me.

"What would Jesus have read about himself in Isaiah?"

Mack gave me a look as if I might regret asking that. "Well, it's not pretty but let's read it:

> Isaiah 52:13-14[NLT]
>
> [13]See, my servant will prosper; he will be highly exalted.
>
> [14]But many were amazed when they saw him. His face was so disfigured he seemed hardly human, and from his appearance, one would scarcely know he was a man."

"And he was *still* willing to go through it all?" I asked in shock.

Mack responded in a more serious tone, "Pretty incredible, huh? He knew that his face and body would be more unrecognizable than any man in history by the time they were done with him. You'll never have to suffer like Christ did but your mission won't always be comfortable either. Remember to lean on Jesus Christ's example of what a man is capable of enduring when you find yourself needing some encouragement to persevere through the hard times."

I knew the road ahead to the Major Leagues would be tough, but having the greatest example of a man on a mission and to grasp what he was able to endure by keeping his mind on God and His Word was inspiring for my own journey.

Mack continued, "That wasn't all he'd have to endure:

> Isaiah 53:7<sup>NLT</sup>
> He was oppressed and treated harshly, yet he never said a word. He was led like a lamb to the slaughter. And as a sheep is silent before the shearers, he did not open his mouth.

"Jesus learned that he would be insulted and treated harshly *and* that **his response to it all would need to be to never fight back physically or verbally**. Jesus' life was threatened from birth [49] and several times throughout his life[50] yet he was instructed to never retaliate," Mack revealed.

I was fired up inside just reading about what he went through, *let alone* having to actually endure it. "How's that possible to take all that without fighting back?"

"He knew he had to fulfill the Scriptures and believed the information God gave him that he would be raised from the dead[51] and exalted more than any man."[52]

"That's incredible. His focus wasn't on him. It was on the end goal – us," I realized. "And to never retaliate *even* once

---

[49] **Matthew 2:13 NIV®:** When they had gone, an angel of the Lord appeared to Joseph in a dream. "Get up," he said, "take the child and his mother and escape to Egypt. Stay there until I tell you, for Herod is going to search for the child to kill him."

[50] **Mark 14:55; Luke 4:29; John 8:59**; to name a few

[51] **Matthew 16:21 NIV®:** From that time on Jesus began to explain to his disciples that he must go to Jerusalem and suffer many things at the hands of the elders, the chief priests and the teachers of the law, and that he must be killed and on the third day be raised to life.

[52] **Philippians 2:8-9 ESV®:** [8]And being found in human form, he humbled himself by becoming obedient to the point of death, even death on a cross. [9]Therefore God has highly exalted him and bestowed on him the name that is above every name,

during the pain and persecution – now *that's* mental toughness."

Mack sat in disbelief with me before saying, "There's a record in 1 Peter that instructs us in how we're to respond in similar situations:

### 1 Peter 2:19-23<sup>WT</sup>

[19]Surely this *is* grace:  when someone who is suffering unjustly endures grief on account of *his* conscience toward God.

[20]In fact, what kind of credit *is it* if you patiently endure when you sin and are buffeted *for it?* However, if you patiently endure when you do good and suffer *for it*, this *is* grace before God.

[21]Moreover, for this purpose you were called, because Christ also suffered for you, leaving an example to you so that you might follow his tracks, [22 Isaiah 53:9:] **'who did not sin, nor was deceit found in his mouth.'**

[23]When he was insulted, he did not retaliate with an insult.  When he suffered, he did not threaten *in return*, but he delivered *himself* to Him Who judges justly."

Sure enough, the second I say I can't do something, God's Word raises the standard showing what's possible through Jesus Christ's example.   "That'll take some real practice but if God says it's possible, it must be possible. Mack, did people not know what Jesus was accomplishing for them?"

"A few understood[53] but most didn't, including those closest to him.[54] Let that be a lesson to you, that it doesn't take having a lot of people believing in your mission for you to complete it.  **Few people will ever *really* grasp the dedication and sacrifice it will take to get to the top and it's not your job to explain yourself or defend your commitment**. There will be plenty of people and obstacles to discourage you.  It happened to Jesus Christ even during his crucifixion.   Yet, he had the mental awareness to never retaliate and *instead* forgave those people because they didn't

---

[53] **Mark 15:43 NIV®:** Joseph of Arimathea, a prominent member of the Council, who was himself waiting for the kingdom of God, went boldly to Pilate and asked for Jesus' body.

[54] **Matthew 16:21-23 NIV®:** [21]From that time on Jesus began to explain to his disciples that he must go to Jerusalem and suffer many things at the hands of the elders, the chief priests and the teachers of the law, and that he must be killed and on the third day be raised to life.  [22]Peter took him aside and began to rebuke him.  "Never, Lord!" he said.  "This shall never happen to you!" [23]Jesus turned and said to Peter, "Get behind me, Satan!  You are a stumbling block to me; you do not have in mind the concerns of God, but merely human concerns."

understand the magnitude of the moment.[55] **He allowed his actions to do the talking. Do the same."**

The insults I had received on the field and on social media paled in comparison to the way Jesus Christ was treated. I determined right then that anytime I felt the hate I could ask myself, *compared to what?* The way Jesus Christ was mistreated, insulted, and assaulted? If Jesus could forgive them for what they did to him and the insults he endured while being crucified,[56] I could learn to endure, ignore, and forgive, too.

"Jacoby, if at some point you choose to make playing for God's glory your *purpose-full* mission, you can expect to receive hate and insults from people, too. Obviously not to the same extent but we already see it in the way the media portrays Christian athletes today. There's nothing new under the sun," Mack reminded me.

"I can tell why the conversation you had with that client was a *game changer.* I'm seeing why a clearly defined mission and purpose helped Jesus endure incredible adversity

---

[55] **Luke 23:34 NIV®:** Jesus said, "Father, forgive them, for they do not know what they are doing." And they divided up his clothes by casting lots.

[56] **Luke 23:39 NIV®:** One of the criminals who hung there hurled insults at him: "Aren't you the Messiah? Save yourself and us!"

on his way to completing his mission that impacted the course of history," I concluded.

"**If you're defining a mission, you might as well design it to have a *lasting impact* and have it be part of your innermost being. The greater the mission, the harder it will be to give up or give in**," he said.

## Checking for Understanding and for Teaching Others

- Jesus had a **clearly defined mission** that gave him purpose as the Savior.

- Jesus **prepared** himself for the mission ahead by reading what he would have to endure:
  - His face and body would be marred (disfigured to the point of unrecognizable) more than any man (Isaiah 52:14).
  - He would be despised and rejected of men (Isaiah 53:3).
  - People would have low esteem of him [disrespect, low opinion, mock] (Isaiah 53:3).

- Jesus **learned how he was to respond to the adversity** he encountered and never retaliated.

- He accomplished it all by believing God's Word and keeping the end goal in mind:
  - He would be raised from the dead (Matt 16:21-23) and exalted (Isaiah 52:13).

- **Mission Accomplished**: God *has* [present tense] highly exalted Christ Jesus; and has given him a name above all names to which every knee *shall* [still future] bow down and confess that Jesus Christ is lord, to the glory of God the Father (Philippians 2:8-11).

## Sport Application

- Having a clearly defined mission and purpose will absolutely benefit you in going all out in pursuit of your end goal.
  - Prepare yourself as much as possible by understanding every aspect of your mission:
    - The mental and physical demands
    - Being away from family and loved ones for long periods of time
    - Poor wages in the minors while trying to support self and family
    - Extreme temperatures and long bus rides
    - Slumps where you feel like you have no clue what you're doing
  - Where your adversity will come from:
    - Your own mind
    - Injuries and setbacks
    - Temptations: Women, money, drugs....
    - Unruly and disrespectful fans and media (home and on the road)
  - What your prize will be for staying committed to the very end and accomplishing your mission
  - Have the mental awareness and sharpness to never retaliate.
- Always keep in mind that you and God make the majority in any situation.

"Did Jesus Christ have the option to give up or give in?"

"Every moment of his life. At any moment he could've gone about accomplishing his own agenda or fallen victim to the pressures he faced, and yet, everything he said[57] and everything he did[58] came from constantly checking in with God. He refused to give into temptation and never sinned once.[59] *That's* **the kind of disciplined commitment and support his mission required**."

"He really kept in touch with God well," I recognized.

"**If you're going to accomplish all that you're setting out to do,** *the mission must come first* **and constantly checking in with God will be a huge support system**. Your mission doesn't care if you're sore, if you're tired, or if you just don't *feel like it* today. **You do what you have to do when you have to do it to get the job done moment by moment and day after day**. Some days will be easier than others but there'll be tough moments that will have you questioning yourself and your mission. Would you like to look at one of the toughest moments in Jesus' life and what he chose to do?"

---

[57] **John 3:34 NLT:** For he is sent by God. He speaks God's words, for God gives him the Spirit without limit.

[58] **John 5:19 ESV®:** So Jesus said to them, "Truly, truly, I say to you, the Son can do nothing of his own accord, but only what he sees the Father doing. For whatever the Father does, that the Son does likewise.

[59] **Hebrews 4:14-15 ESV®:** [14]Since then we have a great high priest who has passed through the heavens, Jesus, the Son of God, let us hold fast our confession. [15]For we do not have a high priest who is unable to sympathize with our weaknesses, but one who in every respect has been tempted as we are, yet without sin.

"Absolutely."

"In Luke 22 there's a record of Jesus Christ going out to pray, knowing that in a just a few moments he would allow himself to be arrested, questioned, mocked, beaten, and killed. In **his moment of greatest need, he chose to pray to God** and asked his disciples to pray with him:

> Luke 22:39-46[NIV®]
>
> [39]Jesus went out as usual to the Mount of Olives, and his disciples followed him.
>
> [40]On reaching the place, he said to them, "Pray that you will not fall into temptation."
>
> [41]He withdrew about a stone's throw beyond them, knelt down and prayed,
>
> [42]"Father, if you are willing, take this cup from me; yet not my will, but yours be done."
>
> [43]An angel from heaven appeared to him and strengthened him.
>
> [44]And being in anguish, he prayed more earnestly, and his sweat was like drops of blood falling to the ground.

<sup>45</sup>When he rose from prayer and went back to the disciples, he found them asleep, exhausted from sorrow.

<sup>46</sup> "Why are you sleeping?" he asked them. "Get up and pray so that you will not fall into temptation."

Looking at the detail in which Jesus was being described caused my heart to hurt. "I don't blame him for asking if there was any other way.  I would've done the same.  But there wasn't, was there?"

Mack shook his head and said in a low tone, "It was the only way.  He prayed this prayer to God two other times just to make sure.  Yet, it had to be done with the sacrifice of his life so he put how he might have felt aside and put the mission first.  Again, disciplined commitment," he pointed out.

I couldn't imagine my parents having to watch me go through something like that.  "It must have really pained God to watch that happen."

"Definitely," he agreed.  "But remember, God knew what Jesus was accomplishing and was well-pleased with him[60] and knew He'd raise him from the dead to sit at His right hand forevermore. That's where God's focus was."

"And I can't believe Jesus' disciples fell asleep on him when he asked them to pray with him."

"They were pretty dedicated throughout his ministry, yet in his hour of greatest need, they were just too emotionally exhausted to stay up and pray with him. But God never left him and sent an angel to strengthen him." Mack paused and looked at me, "**In the hours your mission demands the most of you, you'll need a strong support system to encourage you to stay committed, too**. Men may fail you, but God never will, so you never have to fear anyone or any situation."[61]

"That must have given Jesus a lot of comfort knowing God was always with Him," I added.

"Absolutely. Right after God sent that angel to strengthen him, and just before Jesus allowed himself to be arrested, he revealed that he had the power at any moment to

---

[60] **Isaiah 53:10 KJV**: Yet it pleased the LORD to bruise him; he hath put *him* to grief: when thou shalt make his soul an offering for sin, he shall see *his* seed, he shall prolong *his* days, and the pleasure of the LORD shall prosper in his hand.

[61] **Hebrews 13:5b-6 ESV®**: [5]...for he has said, "I will never leave you nor forsake you." [6]So we can confidently say, "The Lord is my helper; I will not fear; what can man do to me?"

call on God, who was ready to send more than twelve legions of angels (72,000) to rescue him[62] yet he knew in order to complete the mission of salvation he would have to be arrested and allow himself to be killed, which he did, and *earned* the right to say *it is finished*."[63]

I felt a lump growing in my throat. "A fitting end to the greatest mission ever accomplished."

"He isn't done yet. God is sending him back for us someday and everything will be put under his feet except God Himself."[64]

---

[62] **Matthew 26:47 & 53-54 NIV®:** [47]While he was still speaking, Judas, one of the Twelve, arrived. With him was a large crowd armed with swords and clubs, sent from the chief priests and the elders of the people. [53]"Do you think I cannot call on my Father, and he will at once put at my disposal more than twelve legions of angels? [54]But how then would the Scriptures be fulfilled that say it must happen in this way?"

[63] **John 19:30 NIV®:** When he had received the drink, Jesus said, "It is finished." With that, he bowed his head and gave up his spirit.

[64] **1 Corinthians 15:27-28 WT:** [27]for He [*God*] *is to* put all *things* in subjection under his [*Jesus Christ's*] feet. When He says that all *things* have been put in subjection under *him*, it is evident that *it is* with the exception of Him Who put all *things* in subjection under him. [28]When all *things* have been put in subjection under him, then the Son himself will also be subject under Him Who put all *things* in subjection under him [*the Son*], so that God may be all in all.

"Is that when things like death, injuries, pain, and crying will be completely gone?"[65]

"That's right. And in the meantime Jesus is at God's right hand making communication available between us and God.[66] In some branches of Christianity people go through a priest to talk to God, but the Scriptures say that Jesus Christ is our Great High Priest who makes it available to approach God directly and with confidence at any time.[67] Jesus Christ *is still* working today!" Mack emphasized.

---

[65] **Revelation 21:4 KJV**: And God shall wipe away all tears from their eyes; and there shall be no more death, neither sorrow, nor crying, neither shall there be any more pain: for the former things are passed away.

[66] **Romans 8:34 WT**: Who can condemn *them*? Christ? *No, he is* the one who died, and rather who was raised [*from the dead*], who is also at the right *side* of God, *and* who also makes intercession for us.

[67] **Hebrews 4:14-16 NIV®**: [14]Therefore, since we have a great high priest who has ascended into heaven, Jesus the Son of God, let us hold firmly to the faith we profess. [15]For we do not have a high priest who is unable to empathize with our weaknesses, but we have one who has been tempted in every way, just as we are—yet he did not sin. [16]Let us then approach God's throne of grace with confidence, so that we may receive mercy and find grace to help us in our time of need.

### Checking for Understanding and for Teaching Others

- Jesus Christ had a choice every moment to fulfill God's mission of salvation which demanded a perfect sacrifice.
- He chose to fulfill it and always did those things that pleased God knowing that God would never leave him.
- Jesus had an incredible support system in God. He knew he couldn't do it alone and always relied on Him.

### Sport Application

- In order to accomplish your mission **you'll have to do what the mission requires**, not what you feel like doing.
- When things get tough, others may fall away, quit, give in, or give up. Not you!
- In your moments of greatest mental and physical need, pray to God for support.
- Always take comfort knowing God is nearer than your very breath. **Be confident in that and gain confidence from it**.
- Embrace the mission. Triumph over adversity! It's only painful while you're doing it.
- Any pain you endure will pale in comparison to the pleasure you'll feel when you can say, "mission accomplished."
- Push until the mission is complete. Earn the right to say 'it is finished.'

"So if Jesus Christ completed his mission on earth, is there another plan right now until God sends him back for us?" I asked.

"We can find God's *current* desire for the world in 1 Timothy:

1 Timothy 2:3-4<sup>NIV®</sup>

<u>1 Timothy 2:3-4</u>$^{NIV®}$

³This is good, and pleases God our Savior,

⁴who wants all people to be saved and to come to a knowledge of the truth.

"That's a *pretty* lofty vision. How does God expect to accomplish that?"

"With you and me and every other believer out there who chooses to commit their lives to being a representative of Christ," Mack responded. "Jacoby, if you *really* want a *purpose-full* mission worth pursuing, God's invitation to live your life and give your utmost for His Highest is *the* one you'll never regret. He's only got your mouth, your feet, and your hands."

"What value could *I* bring God?" I asked.

"**Look at the cost of what He was willing to pay for your life and then ask how much value God sees in you**. **He was willing to pay for your life with the life of His only begotten son**. There's a verse in Romans written to Christians that details exactly what God asks of us by way of the Apostle Paul:

Romans 12:1-2<sup>WT</sup>

<sup>1</sup>Therefore, brothers, I exhort you by the compassion of God to present your bodies a living sacrifice, holy [*sanctified*], well-pleasing to God, *which is* your logical divine service [*as sons of God*].

"Jacoby, God's not asking you to die for Him. Jesus Christ already did that." Mack explained. "God's asking you to *live* for Him with your entire being in light of all that's been done for you. It's really the least we could do to honor God and Jesus Christ."

"A *living* sacrifice," I said under my breath. "That makes sense. How much good could I do for God if I were dead? So God's hope for each Christian is that they choose to *live* for Christ and share the Gospel?"

"That's what's well-pleasing to Him. Whether it's in pro ball or in any other profession you pursue, you have the choice to live your life with and for God, but it's up to you. He can't make you do anything you don't want to do any more than He could stop Adam from sinning or take the place of Jesus on the cross. Those were choices they chose to make and God's given you the same free will that He gave them."

I thought back to the record in Genesis of God giving Adam specific instructions for his benefit to not eat of that tree and the consequences of doing so, yet he still chose to disobey.[68] Then I thought of Jesus in the garden asking God if there was any other way, to which God knew there wasn't but sent an angel to strengthen him.

Mack continued on, "You see, **everything written in the Bible is inspired by God[69] but not everything in It is God-inspired**. Any good parent understands the best thing they can do is provide their children with guidelines and life lessons that will decrease the likelihood of them experiencing pain or traveling down the wrong path. But they can't make those choices for their children. God is no different. He cannot overstep your free will or stop life from happening to you but He has equipped us with the wisdom of His powerful Word, which contains everything pertaining to life, and a

---

[68] **Genesis 2:16-17 ESV®**: [16]And the Lord God commanded the man, saying, "You may surely eat of every tree of the garden, [17]but of the tree of the knowledge of good and evil you shall not eat, for in the day that you eat of it you shall surely die."

[69] **2 Timothy 3:16-17 KJV**: [16]All Scripture *is* given by inspiration of God, and *is* profitable for doctrine, for reproof, for correction, for instruction in righteousness: [17]That the man of God may be perfect, throughly furnished unto all good works.

relationship with Him to accompany us in navigating this life."[70]

At that moment I realized every decision I'd ever made in life was of my own choosing for good or bad. I'd always thought obeying the Bible would take the joy out of life but not anymore. "I think for the first time I'm seeing that God gave us His Word for our benefit, not our detriment."

Right then I heard the door to Mack's office open with his next client coming in. We had gone over our time but it felt like we had just sat down. I was excited to start *living* for God and His Son Jesus Christ. "You've given me a lot to consider. When I came in today I was aimless and looking for direction. And after what you've just shared with me I feel like I want to live and give my utmost for His Highest. I'm excited to start! Thanks for your time, Mack. I'll see you next week."

"Have a great day, Jacoby, and remember you  chart your path but it's always good to check in with God along the way."[71]

---

[70] **2 Peter 1:3 WT**: His divine power has given us all *things* pertaining to life and godliness through the knowledge [*acknowledgement*] of Him Who called us by His own glory and virtue.

[71] **Proverbs 16:1-3 NIV®**: [1]To humans belong the plans of the heart, but from the Lord comes the proper answer of the tongue. [2]All a person's ways seem

## Checking for Understanding and for Teaching Others

**God's Vision Statement:**

1 Timothy 2:3-4[NIV©]

[3]This is good, and pleases God our Savior,
[4]who wants all people to be saved and to come to a knowledge of the truth.

**God's Mission for You:**

- Jesus Christ sacrificed his life for you and God is asking you to live your life for the one who died for you (Romans 12:1).

**Why make playing for God's glory your *purpose-full* sport *mission*?**

---

pure to them, but motives are weighed by the Lord. [3]Commit to the Lord whatever you do, and he will establish your plans.

# The Perfect Motivation

## Chapter 5

After deciding last week to devote my life and baseball career to playing for God's glory, I felt a new sense of purpose in everything I was doing.  Even physical therapy had taken on a whole new life and meaning as I took on my purpose-full mission.

When I arrived at Mack's office for our fourth session, he greeted me with his signature smile and handshake.  We talked about how week one of my mission was going and I shared with him that I'd been faithful in approaching physical therapy with a good attitude.

"Sounds like you're motivated right now, Jacoby.  That's what good sources of motivation do.  They help bring out the best qualities in you to drive you to accomplish what you're setting out to do."

"I agree. I attacked physical therapy this week like it was my job and I enjoyed it. Since realizing God is the ultimate doctor Who's able to heal me stronger than before I've been approaching physical therapy as a new challenge we're conquering together. I also started reading my Bible too," I said as I showed him I'd brought mine.

"I saw that. Way to take ownership of your spiritual life," Mack commended.

"I might put a Bible app on my phone. Any recommendations?"

Mack handed me his phone with an app pulled up, "I use an app called thebible.org. It shows several versions at once and it's easy to use."

I scrolled down, appreciating the simple layout before handing it back to him. "I like it. So, after last week I had some time to reflect on my new purpose-full mission and realized that the motivations I had before like money, girls, and fame, don't really line up with playing for God. What am I supposed to use for motivation now?"

"There's a record in Hebrews 12 that shows what Jesus used for motivation that we could look at together," Mack suggested.

"Well, if it helped him accomplish the greatest mission of all time, we should probably take a look," I concluded.

"Alright, let's turn to Hebrews chapter 12.

### Hebrews 12:1-3[WT]

[1]Therefore, since we have such a great cloud of witnesses encompassing us, let us strip off every impediment and entangling sin and run with patience *in* the contest lying before *us*,

[2]looking with undivided attention to the leader down the path and perfecter of the [*right way of*] believing, namely, Jesus, who, because of the joy lying before him, endured the cross, disregarding the shame, and sat down at the right *side* of the throne of God.

[3]By all means, attentively consider him who has endured such controversy from sinners against himself, so that you are not weary and exhausted in your souls.

I continued to grow in respect and appreciation of Jesus Christ the more I read about him. His selflessness, his humility, his determination, his endurance, and his self-control were all admirable character traits.  "Mack, what was the joy ahead it mentioned?  It couldn't have been the cross."

"That joy ahead was knowing that you, I and anyone else who chooses to believe on his name would be saved. That's what fueled him," he said before pausing.  "**His ability to stay his mind on the joy ahead while enduring the cross, his having the presence of mind to not retaliate when insulted, and his confidence in God's promise to raise him from the dead we're all character traits that stemmed from his motivation to complete his mission**.  In baseball, whatever you make your motivation will be a deciding factor in how much effort you put forth and how committed you'll be to your Big League pursuit.  Jacoby, Jesus Christ is the *perfect* motivation and example of believing to look to so that you never grow weary in mind during your mission.  **It wasn't about him.  It was all about us**."

"So Jesus was focused on us, and in turn, we're to focus on him?"

"That's right.  Most people setting out to make an impact in the world do it out of self-interest.  Not Jesus.  He had the interests of everyone else in mind when he sacrificed his life, and the more you learn about Jesus Christ, the more Christ-like you'll become in every aspect of your life."

I was beginning to grasp the immense benefit of looking to Jesus as my limitless source of motivation – and whatever I encountered ahead, I could remember it's *nothing* compared to what he endured.

Mack continued, "Jesus never budged. He never fell victim to temptation and never buckled under pressure. He wasn't a pushover. The Bible doesn't say Jesus Christ was a *nice* guy. Jesus did and said what God instructed him to do and say, and sometimes that involved calling people out[72] when they were wrong or flipping tables when they used the Temple as a marketplace,"[73] he remarked.

---

[72] **John 8:42-45 NIV®**: [42]Jesus said to them, "If God were your Father, you would love me, for I have come here from God. I have not come on my own; God sent me. [43]Why is my language not clear to you? Because you are unable to hear what I say. [44]You belong to your father, the devil, and you want to carry out your father's desires. He was a murderer from the beginning, not holding to the truth, for there is no truth in him. When he lies, he speaks his native language, for he is a liar and the father of lies. [45]Yet because I tell the truth, you do not believe me!

[73] **John 2:14-16 NIV®**: [14]In the temple courts he found people selling cattle, sheep and doves, and others sitting at tables exchanging money. [15]So he made a whip out of cords, and drove all from the temple courts, both sheep and cattle; he scattered the coins of the money changers and overturned their tables. [16]To those who sold doves he said, "Get these out of here! Stop turning my Father's house into a market!"

"Mack, Jesus Christ was kind of a bad ass," I had to admit.

"I can't argue with you there. As you read the Gospels and look to him as your primary motivation it will absolutely impact the way you think, the way you play, the way you train, the way you carry yourself on and off the field, and the way you influence the people around you," he said as he reached for a sip of water. "But again, it's up to you what you'll choose as your motivating force; but whatever it is, make sure it gives you the inner drive to bring your best in everything you do."

"That makes sense. What about goal setting, Mack? I've used it for motivation before and sometimes it helps me and sometimes setting goals has added pressure."

"In sport, setting goals *in your control* is a great source of motivation. The added pressure arrives when you set too big a goal or one that's outside your control, like getting a hit. What's easier to do, get a hit or see a ball well?"

"See a ball well, of course."

"And when you're seeing the ball well, what tends to happen?" Mack drilled.

"I tend to hit the ball harder, which leads to more hits."

"Exactly. And which one is completely in your control and repeatable every pitch?"

I needed a pen to write this stuff down. How could I have played baseball this long and never learned something so simple yet so impactful to my success? How many times had I hit a ball hard right at someone and got upset and let it carry into my next at-bat? "So if I keep my goals simple and in my control, it'll be more likely that I get the results I want more consistently?"

"That's right. You can't control whether or not you get a hit but you can absolutely control how well you see the ball. **Keep your goals simple and keep doing simple better**. And, motivation goes so far beyond the playing field and **no one can motivate you but you**. There's three questions I ask athletes to help them get clear on their motivating factor that set the tone for *how* they'll go about their business in sport," he said while putting up three fingers. "***Who are you playing for? Why are you playing for them? And what are you playing for?***"

"Well, if we're starting with question one, my answer would be that I play for God and His Son Jesus Christ. But how can I play for them if in reality I play for a coach?" I said, confused.

Mack reached for a Bible. "Let's look at what God told Paul to write to the believers at Colosse in regards to work, and we can gain some insight as to what it means to play for a coach but really be playing for something bigger in your heart:

> Colossians 3:22-24<sup>NIV®</sup>
>
> [22]Slaves, obey your earthly masters in everything; and do it, not only when their eye is on you and to curry their favor, but with sincerity of heart and reverence for the Lord.
>
> [23]Whatever you do, work at it with all your heart, as working for the Lord, not for human masters,
>
> [24]since you know that you will receive an inheritance from the Lord as a reward. It is the Lord Christ you are serving.

I read it again. So I'd be playing for a coach on the outside but for Christ on the inside. "So, **whenever my coach or organization asks me to do something, I should treat it as if Jesus Christ *himself* is asking me to do it**?"

"Yes. Not just in sport either. In *everything* you do, Jacoby, do it as if Jesus Christ asked you to do it. Whether it's taking out the trash, doing your homework on time, working hard in practice when no one's watching – everything you do, do it as if Jesus Christ asked you to do it. When you begin to take that approach and attitude of integrity in all you do, you'll be doing God's Word and will inevitably become a major asset to whatever organization you're playing for."

"What about when I'm mad at my coaches and just can't find it in me to respect them and do what they ask?" I fired back.

"I'm not saying it's always going to be easy but if God's Word is going to be the standard you set for your life it'll come down to your decision to do what the Word says or not. Remember, let it be the Word of God that motivates you, not the circumstances. If Jesus Christ asked you to do something, you'd never think to slack off or have a bad attitude about it, would you?"

He was right. If God's Word says it's possible for me to respect my coaches like I would Jesus Christ, it *must* be possible. "Sounds pretty hard, Mack. But if God says it can be done, I'm up for the challenge."

"In life and sport you're not always going to like your bosses and coaches. Yet, when you elevate what God's Word says above how you might feel in the circumstances, it then becomes doable to obey what your coach asks you to do with a good attitude. You're not trying to please man. It's Christ you serve," he reminded me.

I didn't know I'd be asked to uphold the standards of God's Word in playing for God but it made sense. "I just know how bitter I can get sometimes when I feel I'm not being respected or treated fairly. You're really asking me to grow, Mack."

"God's Word is asking you to grow, not me. There are benefits to God's approach if you think about it. Scouts and coaches will see how coachable you are and the incredible work ethic you maintain and *that's* what will get you places. But it'll all come back to remembering who you *really* serve," he said.

It hadn't hit me how much *who* I play for impacted *how* I played. By playing for God and serving Jesus Christ the circumstances could constantly change but my attitude and approach could remain the same. I wouldn't be playing to please a coach or to earn playing time. Playing for Jesus Christ in my heart could motivate me to up my work ethic to help me earn playing time and be an addition to my team's success rather than a distraction. "What's the next question again, Mack?"

"The next question is *why* will you play for God's glory?"

It only seemed logical to give my life as a *living* sacrifice in service to the one who died for me. "To be honest, since learning God so loved me that He gave His Son for me I've had a burning desire inside to give everything I've got for Him."

I could tell by Mack's response that I wasn't the first of his clients to say something along those lines after grasping the magnitude of God's love. He shared, "As you continue to grow in your knowledge of all that's been done for you, that burning desire will keep growing. Let me ask you this: How do you feel when your coach puts you in a game situation where he has all the confidence in the world that you'll get the job done?"

"Like I make an important contribution to the team's success," I responded.

"Well, there's a verse in Ephesians where God by way of the Apostle Paul has all the confidence in the heavens that you can get the job done for Him:

<u>Ephesians 4:1</u><sup>ESV®</sup>

I therefore, a prisoner for the Lord, urge you to walk in a manner worthy of the calling to which you have been called,

"What does it mean to walk worthy of the calling?" I asked.

"That phrase *walk (peripateō) worthy (axiōs)* in Greek means to live in balance with or in equal value to all that's been done for you and all that God's made you to be in Christ," he expounded.

How was *I* being invited by the Creator of the Heavens and Earth personally to continue His vision of everyone being saved and coming to a knowledge of the truth?  "I don't think I'll ever be able to balance out what God's done for me but I can give it my best effort.  I'm hardly qualified."

"Do you realize the potential you have in walking this earth representing Christ?" Mack asked.  "Did you know that the devil wouldn't have had Jesus Christ crucified if he knew

God's plan of salvation was to make spirit life available to *all* men?"[74]

I didn't know I was *that* valuable. "So you're saying the devil would rather have Jesus Christ still walking around than a bunch of *Christ-ins*?"

"That's right. Let's read a verse that has taken me a lifetime to believe that'll help you understand just how valuable you are:

John 14:12[KJV]

Verily, verily, I say unto you, He that believeth on Me, the works that *I* do shall *he* do also; and greater *works* than these shall he do; because *I* go unto My Father.

"What did Jesus mean by *greater* works?" I interrupted. "I've read what he did throughout his life. What could be greater?"

"That's what makes this verse so wonderful to believe. And the short version is, while Jesus walked the earth he could

---

[74] **1 Corinthians 2:7-8 NIV®:** [7]No, we declare God's wisdom, a mystery that has been hidden and that God destined for our glory before time began. [8]None of the rulers of this age understood it, for if they had, they would not have crucified the Lord of glory.

only preach that salvation was coming but that it wasn't available *yet*. We read last week about the 3,000 people saved on the day of Pentecost when the gift of holy spirit first became available, and since then, anyone who believes on the name of Jesus Christ is saved and has the promise of eternal life,"[75] he finished.

I had understood the importance of sharing the Word with people but it was at that moment I fully comprehended that *I* had the privilege of sharing the very words of eternal life. "No wonder the devil wouldn't have had Jesus crucified if he knew there would be thousands of Jesus Christs walking around!"

"We're God's first round draft picks and He doesn't make mistakes. The only question *is*, will you play like one?" Mack asked in a challenging tone.

To know that God only has my hands, my feet and my mouth to move the Gospel made me want to get as good at baseball and sharing the Words of life as possible to have the

---

[75] **Romans 10:9-10 NIV®:** [9]If you declare with your mouth, "Jesus is Lord," and believe in your heart that God raised him from the dead, you will be saved. [10]For it is with your heart that you believe and are justified, and it is with your mouth that you profess your faith and are saved.

biggest platform possible. "I feel like I've got an eagle in my chest ready to burst out."

"That's motivation screaming at you," Mack joked. "And you don't need a huge platform. You can share God's Word with anyone at any time. Jacoby, there's no one like you and never will be. No one else has your smile, your laugh, your personality. No one else can make the same impact you can make. What you bring to the world no one else can bring. *That's* how unique and important you are to God and His Team. You have a chance to make an eternal impact every day beyond the scoreboard," he finished.

An hour ago I thought making an impact in the outcome of a game was huge but now it paled in comparison to winning people to Christ and having God be proud He called me to His Team. "That's a perspective changer. My biggest wins in life won't come on the mound. I could have a terrible day of pitching but speak the Word to *one* person and feel like I got the biggest win of the year."

"And it'll be helpful in keeping your performance lows high and your highs low. No matter what happens in a game it's never life or death. But *you* having the boldness to share God's Word with someone to the point that they decide for themselves to believe on Jesus' name or not, now *that's* life or death," he emphasized. "Everything you do from here on out in your public and private life can be for the glory of God if you choose. What you do with your thought life and actions is up to you. But I promise you, aligning your motivation with the motivation that fueled Jesus Christ to accomplish all that he did will absolutely give you the best opportunity to accomplish all that you're setting out to do and give it *purpose*."

"Are there any specific verses you recommend I memorize to share with people?"

"I suggest memorizing Romans 10:9-10.[76] They have the power to give eternal life. *You* have the power to give people the words of eternal life. Is your estimation of *you* rising yet?" Mack said with raised eyebrows.

"If God's estimation of me is that high, it makes sense to start seeing myself the way God sees me and living it, too. A first rounder, not only capable of impacting a game on the

---

[76] **Romans 10:9-10 NIV®**: [9]If you declare with your mouth, "Jesus is Lord," and believe in your heart that God raised him from the dead, you will be saved. [10]For it is with your heart that you believe and are justified, and it is with your mouth that you profess your faith and are saved.

field but also able to make an *eternal* impact on lives off the field," I said with enthusiasm.

"That actually leads us right into the last question. *What will you get out of playing for God's glory?*"

"I feel like we just answered that," I said. "How could there be anything more satisfying than sharing the words of eternal life with someone?"

Mack started flipping the pages of his Bible, "Remember when we read in Colossians 3:23 that by serving the Lord you'll receive an inheritance as a reward? Well, how good would it feel to win a World Series ring?"

"Like the best thing ever," I imagined.

"Well, think of that *times* eternity. As you continue to take a bold stand for the things of God, He's going to reserve for you eternal rewards," Mack added.

"So wait. On top of a guaranteed seat in heaven, I gain eternal rewards for doing my part for God *now*? Who comes up with this stuff?" I said laughing.

"A God who wants the biggest family possible. How's your motivation doing now?"

"It's spilling over.  I wish I could go play right now."

"I do too.  Let's finish with one more thing I think you'll find helpful for when you do get back to playing.  It's an athletic analogy from the Apostle Paul to the Corinthians on how he prepared himself to win people to Christ that I think will resonate with you:

> ### 1 Corinthians 9:24-27<sup>NIV®</sup>
>
> [24]Do you not know that in a race all the runners run, but only one gets the prize?  Run in such a way as to get the prize.
>
> [25]Everyone who competes in the games goes into strict training.  They do it to get a crown that will not last, but we do it to get a crown that will last forever.
>
> [26]Therefore I do not run like someone running aimlessly; I do not fight like a boxer beating the air.
>
> [27]No, I strike a blow to my body and make it my slave so that after I have preached to others, I myself will not be disqualified for the prize.

"Looks like Paul was willing to do *everything* in order to win people to Christ," I said as I read it again.  "And there's his motivation – an everlasting crown."

"Jacoby, some athletes train four years to run a ten second race that they very well might lose. But playing for God's glory will far outweigh any temporary fame, trophy, or accomplishment you'll ever earn in this lifetime. And by adopting the kind of work ethic Paul speaks of here in your athletic career as well as in your personal time in the Scriptures, it's likely you'll have some major victories and crowns in this life, too. It's a win-win situation. There's everlasting satisfaction in receiving a crown that will never fade. You've tasted sweet victory in baseball before and know what it's like to crave another championship; wait until you experience the victory in sharing the Word with someone and they believe unto eternal life. That hunger to win another keeps growing too!" Mack said.

"I can't think of a greater satisfaction in the world," I said as I pictured getting out there and sharing Romans 10:9-10.

"You won't find one. It'll tickle your heart to be doing the Father's business even in those times baseball isn't going well. It'll keep you going," he said. "What were your takeaways from how Paul described his preparation for winning people to Christ?"

"Paul described his training as focused training where he didn't run with uncertainty.  He didn't just go through the motions like a boxer beating the air instead of an opponent.  I like how he described his mental discipline when he trained his body to be in submission to his mind and described it as finding a sparring partner to beat him black and blue so that he could thoroughly learn the craft under game-like conditions, which is a lot more than I could say about my current practice work ethic," I admitted.

"And why was he willing to do all that?"

"To be thoroughly prepared for the chance to share the Gospel and be someone qualified to serve in the things of God.  That's a serious commitment to winning, Mack," I said. "There's a lot I could learn from here."

"Me too.  We'll learn more about Paul next week but to give you an idea of just how committed he was to sharing God's Word and helping people have a relationship with God, the Scriptures say that within two years of Paul starting his ministry all of Asia Minor had *heard* the Word of God,"[77] he said.

---

[77] **Acts 19:8-10 NIV®:** [8]Paul entered the synagogue and spoke boldly there for three months, arguing persuasively about the kingdom of God.  [9]But some of

To hear that *one* man was the driving force behind an entire region of the world hearing God's Word was absolutely inspiring. "It's like he picked right up where Jesus left off. How could one man do all that?"

"His motivation to be a workman for God led to his relentless persistence day after day and year after year in teaching even when many didn't believe. He also taught faithful men who in turn taught others[78] and sure enough, Christianity spread like wildfire in the first century. *That's* how one man can make an impact," Mack emphasized.

I asked myself, "Could I have that kind of relentlessness in baseball and the things of God? Why *not* me?"

Mack interrupted my thought as if he were reading my mind. "Jacoby, what's stopping *you* from having that kind of impact for God? It'll require staying faithful to growing daily

them became obstinate; they refused to believe and publicly maligned the Way. So Paul left them. He took the disciples with him and had discussions daily in the lecture hall of Tyrannus. [10]This went on for two years, so that all the Jews and Greeks who lived in the province of Asia heard the word of the Lord.

[78] **2 Timothy 2:1-2 ESV®:** [1]You then, my child, be strengthened by the grace that is in Christ Jesus, [2]and what you have heard from me in the presence of many witnesses entrust to faithful men, who will be able to teach others also.

in the Scriptures and sharing God's Word with boldness, but why *not* you?"

"I feel like every time we meet you leave me with a lot to consider, and it's easy to see why your client called to thank you for these talks on mission and motivation as being the catalyst to his return and rise in baseball."

"I hope you got some clarity on deciding your motivating factors. Like we've talked about over the past few weeks, the road to the top isn't easy but keeping Jesus Christ's example of endurance ever present in mind will be the perfect motivation as you continue on your path to professional baseball. Sound about enough for today?" he asked.

"Yes. That was awesome. It'll take me a couple days to digest and put into action but I'm excited. Thanks, Mack. See you next week," I said as I walked out beaming and ready to live and give my utmost for His Highest.

## Checking for Understanding and for Teaching Others

External Motivation: Your #1 goal is to **get,** which leads to not being willing to sacrifice *much*. Motivation *to do* dies when you stop getting.

Internal Motivation: Your #1 goal is to **give,** which leads to a willingness to sacrifice *everything* with no expectation of getting anything in return.

- God so *loved* that He **gave** His only Son = Motivated intrinsically by love (John 3:16).

  o **Reward**: Received many sons and daughters into His family that continues to grow every day.

- Jesus Christ so *loved* that he **gave** his life = Motivated intrinsically by the joy ahead (Hebrews 12:2).

  o **Reward**: God raised him from the dead to die no more and sat Him at His own right hand forevermore to make intercession for us.

## Sport Application

- Compete to win immediate and eternal rewards (I Corinthians 9:24).

- Go into strict training of the mind and body for victory (I Corinthians 9:25).

- Train with purpose to win instead of only going through the motions (I Corinthians 9:26).

- Have the self-discipline to do whatever it takes to learn your craft thoroughly (I Corinthians 9:27).

What do you want God to say about the way you lived your life for Him?

What do you want to accomplish for God's glory?

What do you need to start doing TODAY to begin living that reputation?

# Your *True* Identity

## Chapter 6

A week had passed since our last session and my new motivation for life, sport, and studying God's Word was increasing. But, on the morning of our next session I woke to a text with an article link about my chances of getting drafted next week. My heart sank as I read how scouts had all but written me off due to my injury. Things only grew worse after reading the comments at the bottom of the article. The more opinions I read, the more I started believing them.

Mack could tell something was off the second I stepped into his office. "Jacoby, what's going on?"

I handed him my phone with the article. "Maybe they're right, Mack. Maybe I can't come back from this...."

"Jacoby, if you're going to entertain every opinion about you and allow others to dictate who you are and what you're capable of, how do you ever expect to last in baseball or move God's Word?" Mack challenged.

Until that point I didn't realize I had a choice, as all my life I'd allowed the sports world to dictate who I was and how good I could be. "I've never considered that, I guess."

"I don't like talking about myself because these sessions aren't about me, but when I feel I have something of value to offer from my career, I share it," Mack said taking a sip of water. "After high school I accepted a scholarship to play baseball and a month into fall ball I tore the labrum in my right shoulder. It cost me a year in recovery, just like you."

"Dang. I didn't know that. So you know what I'm going through?"

"Yes. It was the hardest thing to be without the game I loved," he recollected. "And why I'm sharing this with you *now* is to tell you that in some ways it ended up being one of the greatest growth periods of my life."

"What do you mean?"

"Being without baseball allowed me to step back and evaluate my priorities in life, and what I found was that my relationship with God was no longer one of them. It's still hard to admit but I had allowed baseball to become my god, and it took me *not* having the game and experiencing the neglect from coaches and teammates to really cling to God and take ownership of my relationship with Him. Baseball had become my entire identity and without it I felt worthless. That's when I learned the hardest lesson of all." He paused. **"Baseball is what you *do*; it's not who you *are*."**

We sat in silence as those words sunk in. Baseball is what I do. It's not who I am. No wonder I had let that article and the comments from random people beat me down. It hadn't occurred to me just how much I'd gotten wrapped up in my athletic identity. Could this be *my* opportunity to gain proper perspective of my identity? "So Mack, in hindsight, you're glad that injury happened because it helped you become a better player when you got back?"

Mack chuckled. **"I definitely wasn't *glad* it happened but I'm pleased with how I chose to respond by investing my time in areas that helped me mature as a man and as a ballplayer."**

"What did you do for that year?"

"I found new hobbies and did all the fun things I rarely got to do growing up because of my dedication to sports. But the most important investment I made was time in God's Word. My world was shattered when I learned how fragile my athletic career could be and I vowed to never again be defined by what I did on the field. So I went to the One Source I knew would give me the *truth* of who I was – God's Word," he said.

"What'd you read that filled that void?"

"I'll show you because it applies to you, too. Grab your Bible and turn with me to 1 John.

> 1 John 3:1-2<sup>WT</sup>
>
> [1]Behold what manner of love the Father has given to us that we should be called children of God (and *so* we are). Because of this, the world does not know us because it did not know Him. [2]Beloved, we are children of God now, and (*although* it has not yet been revealed what we shall be) we know that when he [*Jesus Christ*] is revealed, we shall be like him, for we shall see him as he is.

Mack continued, "I still remember the first time I read that God loved me and that I was His child *now*. At the time I didn't feel loved by teammates or coaches and I certainly didn't feel lovable. I felt lost and alone. But, it was the

Scriptures that showed me my true identity and released me from the shackles of caring what other people thought of me."

I had put so much pressure on myself to be who others wanted me to be that I no longer had a healthy understanding of who *I* wanted to be.  But after reading those verses that *I* am a child of God I felt wanted and valuable again.

Mack stood up and moved towards a globe to spin it and said, "The sports world will have many opinions of you, depending on how you're performing, but God's truth about you as His child will always remain the same.  **Whether you choose to see yourself as a baseball player who happens to be Christian or a Christian who happens to play baseball will be *your* decision every day**."

"What's the difference?"

"The ballplayer who happens to be Christian still allows the world to dictate who he is and what he's worth depending on how he's playing.  That's a roller coaster you don't want to ride.  But the Christian who happens to play baseball has the freedom to find peace in who the Word says he is regardless of how he's currently performing.

## Checking for Understanding and for Teaching Others

- The world will come at you from multiple angles.
- God will only come at you from one, truth.
- Once you believe Romans 10:9-10 you forever become a child of God (1 John 3:1-2)

For you, what's the difference in being an athlete first and a Christian second, and vice versa?

## Sport Application

- Due to the amount of time you spend in your sport it will become your god if you let it
- Establish your identity or the world will choose one for you.
- Failing to develop a strong identity outside of sport will leave you feeling worthless when you temporarily or permanently leave sport.
- Do not play to the expectations of others – you can't win that war.

Who are you outside of sport?

What problems do you foresee with having an identity heavily wrapped up in sport?

It seemed I had two identity choices. I could either see myself through the lenses of the Word or the sports world. The answer seemed obvious but not necessarily easy. "Was it difficult to keep your Christian identity first when you returned to sport?"

"I'm not sure *difficult* is the right word but **making the decision every day to believe what the Word says of you rather than what the sports world says about you will take effort because the world won't remind you of your Christian identity.** It's more likely that you'll be pressured to doubt your identity in Christ. Let's take a look at a great example of this in the Gospel of Matthew where the devil tries to get Jesus to question his identity as the Son of God:

> Matthew 3:16-17[ESV®]
> ¹⁶And when Jesus was baptized, immediately he went up from the water, and behold, the heavens were opened to him, and he saw the Spirit of God descending like a dove and coming to rest on him; ¹⁷and behold, a voice from heaven said, "This is my beloved Son, with whom I am well pleased."

"That must have been pretty encouraging for Jesus to hear God call him His Son," I said in admiration.

"Absolutely. And whether God speaks it like he does here or has it written down like He did for us in 1 John, it's every bit as true because it's from God. Let's keep reading.

Matthew 4:1-3<sup>ESV®</sup>

¹Then Jesus was led up by the Spirit into the wilderness to be tempted by the devil.

²And after fasting forty days and forty nights, he was hungry.

³And the tempter came and said to him, "If you are the Son of God, command these stones to become loaves of bread."

"*When* did the tempter approach Jesus?" Mack asked.

"When he had just gotten done fasting for forty days and would've been at his weakest."

"And what had God *just* got done telling him?"

"That he was His Beloved Son in whom He was well pleased." Then it hit me, "Knowing your identity must really be valuable if that's the *first* thing the devil tempted Jesus to doubt!"

"I think you're on to something. Let's keep reading to see how Jesus responded as an example of how we should respond when our identity as sons of God is being questioned:

Matthew 4:4<sup>ESV®</sup>

But he answered, "It is written, 'Man shall not live by bread alone, but by every word that comes from the mouth of God.'"

"He responded with the Word," I noticed.

"It's the best defense and that's what we're to do as well. We need to know what the Word says of us so we don't get talked out of it. Let's keep reading as the devil wasn't going away that easily:

Matthew 4:5-7<sup>ESV®</sup>

<sup>5</sup>Then the devil took him to the holy city and set him on the pinnacle of the temple

<sup>6</sup>and said to him, "If you are the Son of God, throw yourself down, for it is written, 'He will command his angels concerning you,' and 'On their hands they will bear you up, lest you strike your foot against a stone.'"

<sup>7</sup>Jesus said to him, "Again it is written, 'You shall not put the Lord your God to the test.'"

"The devil questioned his identity *again* and even used Scripture this time!" I said in shock. "But Jesus didn't budge and stuck to the Word again."

"The devil was willing to use any means possible to get Jesus to doubt his identity as the Son of God including the misapplication of the Scriptures. He knows them well and how to subtly twist them by taking out a word here and adding a word there or removing them from their context to where it's no longer God's Word. That's what he did here in quoting Psalm 91:11-12," Mack enlightened.

It struck me how important it would be to equip myself with what God's Word says about me. "Mack, why did the devil want Jesus Christ to question his identity so badly?"

"Had Jesus Christ for a moment lost sight of who he was as the Son of God, he would have lost sight of his mission as the Savior of the world, which was the devil's goal. If you lose sight of your *Christ-in* identity, it's likely you'll be willing to compromise on everything else, too. When you no longer see yourself the way God sees you, how will you rise up to believe that you're a superconqueror in Christ,[79] encourage other Christians, or share the words of eternal life with others?"

---

[79] Romans 8:37 WT: "On the contrary, in all these *things*, we are superconquerors through him who loved us."

Mack had a good point. If I was so focused on what others were saying about me rather than on the spirit that abides in me, how could I ever rise to be who God's made me to be? In baseball, how can I ever be confident in my abilities if I allow the situation or other people to tell me what I'm capable of achieving? "So Mack, **the second I forget who I am is the second I start becoming someone I'm not**?"

"Bingo. Your identity is the foundation everything else is built on. In baseball, when you feel good about yourself, you tend to perform better. In life, when you remember you're more than a conqueror in God's eyes, you tend to live that way. Let's keep reading.

> Matthew 4:8-11<sup>ESV®</sup>
>
> [8]Again, the devil took him to a very high mountain and showed him all the kingdoms of the world and their glory.
>
> [9]And he said to him, "All these I will give you, if you will fall down and worship me."
>
> [10]Then Jesus said to him, "Be gone, Satan! For it is written, 'You shall worship the Lord your God and him only shall you serve.'"
>
> [11]Then the devil left him, and behold, angels came and were ministering to him.

"Did you see what the devil did when Jesus wouldn't fold under *pressure?*" Mack asked.

"He tried to bait him with *pleasures,*" I noticed.

"Exactly. If he can't get us to fold under pressure, he'll try to lure us with pleasures," Mack said. "It could be through money, expensive toys, women, social media – anything to keep you from believing God and His Word. If you're distracted from God, it's likely you'll be distracted from your mission for Him, too."

"So, the devil is willing to give a little in order to gain a lot back in return?"

"That's one of his strategies. He'll present something alluring to tempt us but there's never anything good that comes from it. He's like a fisherman willing to give up a worm to catch a fish by subtly disguising his hook with flashy bait. Many fall for it and get hooked. His favorite catch is a Christian that gets caught up in the things of the world rather than remain in the things of God's Word."

That image resonated with me as I'd been fishing a few times and noticed the good fishermen had the best bait. "I'm glad Jesus saw right through all those temptations."

**"He was prepared with the Word of God, knew who he was, knew the devil's strategies and motives, and was relentless in his pursuit of his mission as the Savior of the world**. As you continue to prepare yourself by studying the Scriptures and see what great value you hold from God's perspective, it will get harder and harder to get talked out of your identity and mission," Mack stated. "Jesus Christ said in John 10:10 that the devil has one goal, which is to steal, to kill and to destroy.[80] When someone tries to steal something from you, what must you have?"

"Something of great value," I said immediately.

"Exactly, and as you keep John 14:12 in mind, that you can do the same works Jesus Christ did and greater works because he ascended to the Father, you'll continue to understand why the devil has no greater fear than to see you walk in God's power."

I paused to let that set in and reminded myself of the major role I could play in raising someone from spiritual death!

---

[80] **John 10:10 ESV®:** The thief comes only to steal and kill and destroy. I came that they may have life and have it abundantly.

I now understood why the devil would be my personal adversary.[81]

Mack kept talking. "The moment you forget your value and the impact you can make in this world for God is the moment the devil doesn't have to worry about you anymore. Remember Jesus' example of how he defended himself with the Scriptures so that you never budge," he said.

"That's like spiritual warfare!" I said.

"That's exactly what it is and you can't win alone. By remaining strong in the lord and in the power of his might you'll be able to withstand the strategies of the devil.[82] Keep in mind, he'll do it in subtle and indirect ways, but he only has one goal and that's to get you to think less of yourself than

---

[81] **1 Peter 5:8-10 WT**: [8]Be sober. Be watchful. Your adversary, the slandering devil, walks about as a roaring lion, seeking whom he may devour. [9]Resist him, *being* firm in the [*right way of*] believing, knowing that the same *kinds* of sufferings are being experienced by *members of* your brotherhood in the world. [10]The God of all grace, Who called you to His eternal glory in Christ [/]Jesus [-], after that you have suffered a little *while*, will Himself fully equip, establish, strengthen you *and* give *you* a firm foundation.

[82] **Ephesians 6:10-13 WT**: [10]Henceforth, be strong in the lord and in the strength of his ability. [11]Clothe yourselves with the full armor of God so that you are able to stand against the strategies of the devil, [12]because to us the wrestling is not against flesh and blood but against the rulers, against the authorities, against the world rulers of this *present* darkness, against the spirits of wickedness in the heavenly *realm*. [13]Wherefore take up the full armor of God so that you are able to resist *those things* in the day of the wicked, and when you have accomplished everything, to stand.

who you really are.  Are you grasping the importance of knowing your identity now?"

I was and I knew it would be my responsibility to understand the strategies he was using to distract me from my relationship with God.  I never again wanted to lose sight of who I was in Christ and what I was capable of doing for God.  "Mack, how will I know all the ways the devil will try to trick me?"

"You don't need to know all his strategies.  You just need to know the genuine Word of God and it'll be easy to spot his counterfeit attempts.  When the devil came at Jesus Christ with a half-truth by manipulating Scripture, Jesus wasn't fazed because he knew the genuine Word of God.  When you invest time into learning the Scriptures, you'll be able to spot the strategies of the devil, too," he instructed.

That seemed like a much better strategy. "That makes sense.  I'll just need to be sharp on the Word."

"And **just because the media slanders your name or something goes bad, don't immediately assume it's the devil causing it**. People will have their opinions of you and things won't always go your way."

## Checking for Understanding and for Teaching Others

- Jesus Christ knew who he was as God's Beloved Son and knew his mission as the Savior of the world.
- The devil questioned his identity first with pressures, then with pleasures.
- Jesus was prepared with the greatest defense ever: "It is written."
- Had Jesus Christ budged on his identity he would have compromised his mission.
- As you continue to take a bold stand for God's glory, your *Christ-in* identity will be challenged every day through pressures and pleasures, especially when you're vulnerable.
- Know your identity in Christ. Realize your value. Stick to your mission. Be strong in the lord and in the strength of his ability to prevail (Ephesians 6:10).

## Sport Application

In sport, what sources will try to talk you out of your identity or get you to compromise?


What are your fishhooks that could lure you away from your *purpose-full* sport mission?


What strategies will you use to avoid getting "hooked"?


"Let's look at one more way you might get talked out of your *Christ-in* identity that has to do with pride and ego. Did you know the devil's original name was Lucifer, which means *the morning star,* and he was second in command to God?" Mack asked.

"Really? I didn't know that."

"God had created him so beautiful that he allowed his pride and ego to get the best of him and began exalting himself rather than his Creator.[83] When he thought he could be like the Most High and rebelled against God with one-third of the angels, God kicked him out of heaven.[84] The Word doesn't mention God hating many things but pride is one of them."[85]

"I didn't know God hated *anything.* What God hates I'm guessing I should hate, too," I realized.

---

[83] **Isaiah 14:12-15 NIV®:** [12]How you have fallen from heaven, morning star, son of the dawn! You have been cast down to the earth, you who once laid low the nations! [13]You said in your heart, "I will ascend to the heavens; I will raise my throne above the stars of God; I will sit enthroned on the mount of assembly, on the utmost heights of Mount Zaphon. [14]I will ascend above the tops of the clouds; I will make myself like the Most High." [15]But you are brought down to the realm of the dead, to the depths of the pit.

[84] **Ezekiel 28:17 NIV®:** Your heart became proud on account of your beauty, and you corrupted your wisdom because of your splendor. So I threw you to the earth; I made a spectacle of you before kings.

[85] **Proverbs 8:13 KJV:** The fear of the LORD is to hate evil: pride, and arrogancy, and the evil way, and the froward mouth, do I hate.

"We should also love what God loves and one of those is humility. God knows that every man needs recognition and as we humble ourselves to Him, He promises to exalt us.[86]

"Mack, from what you've been sharing with me over the past couple weeks I've realized if anyone's deserving of glory or praise, it's God and His Son. Not us."

"I agree. But I want you to be aware of **how important it is to separate who you are from what you do, because being an elite athlete opens a huge door to start glorifying yourself rather than your Creator who gave you your ability in the first place.** You'll be hailed a god in the eyes of fans for your baseball abilities. There's nothing wrong with people admiring you and wanting your autograph but if you don't keep your ego and pride in check, they'll certainly get the best of you and lead you to stray from who you *really* are as a son of God and your mission for God's glory," Mack warned.

I realized how true that was. Over the past few months in high school alone I had already been getting plenty of

---

[86] **1 Peter 5:5-7 ESV®:** [5]Likewise, you who are younger, be subject to the elders. Clothe yourselves, all of you, with humility toward one another, for "God opposes the proud but gives grace to the humble." [6]Humble yourselves, therefore, under the mighty hand of God so that at the proper time he may exalt you, [7]casting all your anxieties on him, because he cares for you.

accolades and attention. "I'd be lying if I said I haven't experienced a bit of ego of late. But my injury knocked me right back down," I said, poking some fun at myself.

Mack laughed with me. "Hey, before we close out today's session let's look at an example in the book of Acts where two Apostles, Paul and Barnabas, were put in a situation where they had the opportunity to glorify themselves or God:

> Acts 14:6-7<sup>WT</sup>
>
> [6]they, being aware of it, fled to Lystra and Derbe, cities of Lycaonia, and to the surrounding region, [7]and there they proclaimed the gospel.

"So right from the start, what was their mission in Lystra and Derbe?" he asked.

"To proclaim the gospel."

"Keep that in mind as we keep reading:

> Verses 8-13<sup>WT</sup>
>
> [8]Now at Lystra, *there* sat a certain man, impotent in his feet, *who was* lame from his mother's womb *and* who had never walked.

$^9$This *man* heard Paul as he was speaking, who, after looking intently at him [*the lame man*] and perceiving that he had believing to be saved [*delivered*],

$^{10}$said with a loud voice, "Stand upright on your feet," and he leaped up and walked.

$^{11}$When the crowds saw what Paul had done, they lifted up their voice, saying in the Lycaonian *language*, "The gods have come down to us in the likeness of mankind."

$^{12}$They called Barnabas, "Zeus," and *they called* Paul, "Hermes," because he was the chief speaker.

$^{13}$Then the priest of Zeus (whose [*temple*] was before the city) brought oxen and garlands unto the gates and desired to offer a sacrifice with the crowds.

"Looks like they had a choice here, didn't they?" Mack asked.

"Yah, they could allow themselves to be glorified as gods or they could give the glory to the One True God," I said.

"Let's see their response:

Verses 14-15[WT]

[14]When the apostles, Barnabas and Paul, heard *about it*, they tore their mantles and rushed out to the crowd crying out

[15]and saying: "Gentlemen, why are you doing these *things*? We also are men of like passions with you, and we are proclaiming the gospel to you so that you turn from these futile *things* unto the living God, Who made the heaven and the earth and the sea and everything that is in them."

"What a humble response!" I thought to myself. "Mack, they could've taken all the credit and been praised as gods but they chose to give the *living God* the glory instead. That's easy to read but I bet it was hard to pass up."

"It really depended on where they put their focus. On them or on God who gave them the ability to heal that man. Paul understood he was able to perform that miracle based on that man's believing and God's ability to heal," he said.

"So Paul was like the middle man?"

"That's right. He couldn't have performed that miracle without receiving information from God to do so and he didn't lose sight of that," Mack explained. "**Had Paul allowed what he _did_ in performing the miracle to go to his head and define who he was (a miracle worker of his own power), he very well might have embraced the _god_-like title the Lycaonians were ready to give him**."

"I liked Paul and Barnabas' humility in recognizing they were _simply_ men like the rest of them and encouraged them to turn to the One True God. I bet some of those people started believing in God after hearing the Word and seeing that miracle," I concluded.

"I bet you're right. Let's bring this back to your career to finish. **Remember to separate what you do from who you are**. As an elite athlete at any level, people will put you on a pedestal and listen to your every word like it's gold. Remember to stay humble to who you are and to your mission even when the temptation to stray comes – and it will come. Don't allow yourself to get caught up in the fame, prestige, money, or titles. Those things pale in comparison to the things God has in store for you. Pride will be your downfall[87]

---

[87] **Proverbs 16:18 ESV®**: Pride goes before destruction, and a haughty spirit before a fall.

but humility will lead to great rewards.[88] Remember sport is just one of your vehicles for spreading the gospel and when you're speaking the Word, keep an ear open to God, who might give you specific instructions to carry out like He did to Paul. You have the capacity to do miracles just like Paul did when God gives you the green light to do so. So always be listening."

That blew my mind to think I could work miracles with the same ability Paul did because it's the same spirit at work within me that was within him. "Thanks for showing me my true identity and how I need to see myself the way God sees me. I'm not letting that article or those comments define me anymore. It's God's opinion of me that matters. Not man's."

---

[88] **Proverbs 22:4 NIV®**:  Humility is the fear of the Lord; its wages are riches and honor and life.

## Checking for Understanding and for Teaching Others

- God hates pride and arrogance (Proverbs 8:13).
- Rather than exalt yourself, humble yourself and allow God to exalt you in due time (1 Peter 5:5-6).

## Sport Application

- Pride is the quickest way to ending your own career. No coach likes it. No one likes it.
- Pride is man's greatest weakness.
- Humility is one of the greatest strengths to develop and the surest way to grow.
- You're not bigger than the game. Be humble to the game or it will humble you.
- Remember who you represent in your heart and you won't get carried away with who you represent on your jersey.
- You never know whose life you might change on any given day. Be the middle man between them and God by giving them the words of life as a representative of Christ.
- Take five minutes a day to visualize opportunities where you'll have the choice to glorify yourself or God and how you'd like it to go.

How will you stay humble to the game and your mission for God's glory when the temptation to elevate your abilities and accomplishment arises (while still taking credit for your hard work and preparation)?

# Committed to the Comeback

## Chapter 7

Sure enough, the June Draft came and went without calling my name. I wasn't surprised but it still stung. Despite the disappointment, I was determined to stay strong and not allow it to define me. *I* wasn't a failure. I just failed to get drafted, just like thousands of other players around the country. I knew I'd get my chance again and was committed to a major comeback.

The first part of summer seemed to fly by with major progress in physical therapy. In two weeks I'd be leaving for summer school at my new university to get acquainted with campus life and hopefully meet some new people. I was grateful to Mack for all he had done in helping me build a strong foundation mentally and spiritually and I'd miss our time together.

Although I had solidified my mission and motivation, there were still lingering doubts as to whether I could really make that big of an impact for God.  Walking into Mack's office for our second to last session I needed some encouragement that God still wanted me on His Team after keeping Him a second stringer to baseball most of my life.

When I pulled up to Mack's office building, he was outside catching some sunshine as he waved me into a parking spot.  We shook hands and walked into his office to get started.  "Mack, I've got to say, it stings that I didn't get drafted but if you told me six weeks ago I'd take it this well, I'd call you crazy.  But, I know I'll have my chance at it again."

"Now that's the kind of attitude that'll get you back to where you want to be the fastest.  And it sounds like you're headed off to college in a few weeks for summer school?" he asked.

"Yah, I'm excited.  I'll miss our talks but I'm ready to start my new adventure," I said as I settled into the familiar chair surrounded by some of my heroes lining the walls.  "Something's been bothering me a bit this week that I was hoping we could discuss."

"Sure.  What's going on?"

"Well, last week you mentioned it took you getting injured to realize you had made baseball your god. I thought about that on my drive home and I came to the realization that I've done the same thing. God's never been number one in my life," I admitted. "And possibly not even number two."

"It's a tough pill to swallow once you become aware of it," Mack empathized. "But now that you *are* aware of it you have the choice to continue seeing yourself as a ballplayer first and a Christian second who makes time for God when it's convenient *or* you can prioritize your relationship with God and make everything else secondary. Remember, whichever identity you choose will set your perspective for how you approach everything else."

"Is there a way to combine the two? I just don't see how I can keep God first and baseball at least second when so much of my time is wrapped up in sport," I said honestly.

Mack understood what I was saying. "You don't have to separate the two. Every workout, every practice, and every game can be a time for you to grow with God by talking with Him and incorporating Scripture into your routines."

I hadn't thought of building my relationship with God as I built my baseball career and immediately liked the idea. "I always thought I had to compartmentalize my spiritual life from everything else. But I guess God can't be put in a box so it makes sense to walk and talk with Him wherever I am. There's another question that's been lingering in my mind this week. You may think is silly after all we've discussed, but after putting God in second place for so long how do I know He still wants me on His Team?"

"Let me ask you this. When you were born, whose child were you?"

"My parents' child, of course."

"And as you got older and became a bit more rebellious at times, whose child were you?"

"Still theirs."

"So," Mack leaned in, "even when you mess up and feel like you don't deserve the love of your parents, are you still their child?"

"Yes. I'm always my parents' child no matter what." Then it clicked. "Wait – so you're saying that's how God's love works, too?"

Mack smiled, seeing my face light up as I put it together. "Many Christians are unsure about their salvation and think it's based on their daily actions. But it's not like playing time in sports where if you're playing well, you're in and if you're not, you're out. Remember, it has nothing to do with what we've done and *everything* to do with what God by way of Jesus Christ *did* for us.[89] Let's look at a parable Jesus Christ spoke that I think will help you see things clearer."

"What's it about?" I asked.

"In the parable the younger of two sons asks his father for his inheritance early, to which the father agrees. He then goes and irresponsibly spends it all like someone might do in Vegas. After losing everything and hitting rock bottom he remembers his father. Let's pick it up there:

> ### Luke 15:17-24[NKJV®]
> [17]"But when he came to himself, he said, 'How many of my father's hired servants have bread enough and to spare, and I perish with hunger!

---

[89] **Ephesians 2:8-10 WT**: [8]By grace, you have certainly been saved [*delivered*] through believing, and this [*salvation*] is not from yourselves. *It is* the offering of God. [9]*It is* not of *our* works so that no one may boast, [10]for we are His workmanship, created in Christ Jesus on the basis of good works that God previously prepared, so that we may walk in them.

$^{18}$I will arise and go to my father, and will say to him, 'Father, I have sinned against heaven and before you,

$^{19}$and I am no longer worthy to be called your son. Make me like one of your hired servants.'

$^{20}$"And he arose and came to his father. But when he was still a great way off, his father saw him and had compassion, and ran and fell on his neck and kissed him.

$^{21}$And the son said to him, 'Father, I have sinned against heaven and in your sight, and am no longer worthy to be called your son.'

$^{22}$"But the father said to his servants, 'Bring out the best robe and put *it* on him, and put a ring on his hand and sandals on *his* feet.

$^{23}$And bring the fatted calf here and kill *it,* and let us eat and be merry;

$^{24}$for this my son was dead and is alive again; he was lost and is found.' And they began to be merry."

"I've heard this one before. The parable of the prodigal son," I recalled. "But when reading, it was the incredible response of the father that stuck out to me."

"Yes, most people know this as the return of the prodigal son. But, I call it the parable of the forgiving father. In Bible times **a parable was used to emphasize a single point and the point of this parable was to highlight the father's loving response towards his son**," he noted. "Did you notice how the son's mistakes drove him to feel unworthy to be called his father's son?"

"Yes. But he got desperate enough to return home and the response of his father was incredible," I said as I picked up my Bible. "In verse 20 it said, 'But when he was still a great way off, his father saw him' – it's like his father was patiently anticipating his return, and when he did, his father didn't scold him or question his decisions. He had compassion and love for him. Wait, I get it now! *That's* the loving response God will have towards me every time I choose to come back to Him no matter how far I feel I've fallen, isn't it?"

"You got it!" Mack said with a smile. "Many Christians and unbelievers alike fear they've messed up beyond God's ability to forgive but that's not the case. God is always willing to meet us where we're at, forgive us, and welcome us back with unconditional love. That's something you'll need to remember every day. In baseball, there will be days where you're just terrible on the mound and that's when you'll need to get good at forgiving yourself and then move forward. The last thing you'll need is a self-inflicted verbal beat down but you'll be tempted to do it."

"Yah, I could definitely use some work on that," I said as I recalled some of the names I've called myself in the past after mistake pitches, and believed them.

"There will also be plenty of times you'll mess up in your personal life so bad that you'll be tempted to hide from God instead of run towards Him," he warned me. "We saw that with Adam and Eve when they hid themselves from God after disobeying, remember?"

"I guess man's been doing it ever since."

"And that's when we need Him the most," Mack encouraged. "He asks us to come boldly to Him. *Not* timidly. Especially when we need help.[90] Jacoby, remember last week when we talked about the importance of separating who you are from what you do?"

"Of course."

---

[90] **Hebrews 4:16 NASB**: Therefore let us draw near with confidence to the throne of grace, so that we may receive mercy and find grace to help in time of need.

"Well, in baseball, how do you feel after a strike-out, an error, or a misplaced pitch that gets shelled?"

"Angry at myself."

"Now, in those moments is it your performance that's bad or *you* that's bad?"

"What's the difference?"

"One is performance based and the other is personal. In sport and life you'll make plenty of mistakes but *you* are never a mistake, regardless of what anyone might tell you or how you might feel in the moment. Does that make sense?"

"That's like in the parable where the son *felt* unworthy to be called his father's son after making a bunch of mistakes. But those mistakes didn't change the fact that he was still his father's son."

"Exactly. It was his decisions that were in error but it didn't make *him* unworthy of his father's love," Mack expounded. "In sport, learning to keep your performance separate from becoming personal will help you recover much quicker and prepare for the next pitch or next game with full confidence. And knowing your sonship with God is sealed and unaffected by anything you do in this life will help you approach Him with confidence."

My appreciation towards God continued to grow as I began to grasp that I didn't have to *already* be good in order to gain His affection and attention. How refreshing to realize that an error doesn't change who I am. **I'm not my performance**. "Either way I don't like making mistakes. But I know they're going to happen and I'll just need to figure out a way to forgive myself and move on to the next pitch."

"Part of what I do is help athletes build routines that allow them to move past their mistakes on the field by **acknowledging** what went wrong, **adjusting** their mindset back to the present moment, and **attacking** the next play with confidence. It takes practice to become habit but once you've got it, you can easily move on and prepare for the next pitch guilt-free. In life, when we screw up and go to God for forgiveness, He not only forgives our mistakes, He forgets them too,"[91,92] Mack said confidently.

I thought to myself how nice would it be to be able to forget a mistake. "Well, if God's not holding on to my screw ups, I guess I shouldn't either!" I realized.

"And I'll let you in on a secret. Except for Jesus Christ, no one's perfect in this life and God knows that better than anyone. In those moments on the field where you feel small, your routines will guide you in getting back to thinking big. In life, the best way to get your focus off your faults is to get it onto God's bountiful grace and mercy."[93]

"I've heard those words grace and mercy before. What do they mean?"

---

[91] **Psalm 103:10-14 ESV®:** [10]He does not deal with us according to our sins, nor repay us according to our iniquities. [11]For as high as the heavens are above the earth, so great is his steadfast love toward those who fear him; [12]as far as the east is from the west, so far does he remove our transgressions from us. [13]As a father shows compassion to his children, so the Lord shows compassion to those who fear him. [14]For he knows our frame; he remembers that we are dust.

[92] **Hebrews 8:12 NIV®:** "For I will forgive their wickedness and will remember their sins no more."

[93] **Romans 3:22-24 KJV:** [22]Even the righteousness of God *which is* by faith of Jesus Christ unto all and upon all them that believe: for there is no difference: [23]For all have sinned, and come short of the glory of God; [24]Being justified freely by his grace through the redemption that is in Christ Jesus:

"*Grace* means undeserved favor. We didn't deserve God's favor but He chose to give it to us anyway. M*ercy* is a withholding of judgment or punishment when we *do* deserve it. The Apostle Paul is a great example of someone who never lost sight of God's grace throughout his life. In every Epistle God had him write he opens by mentioning grace," he noted.

"Why would the Apostle Paul of all people need to be reminded of God's grace?" I asked bewildered. "After reading about his commitment to moving God's Word I was inspired all week."

## Checking for Understanding and for Teaching Others

- In a parable many points may be made but only one aspect is emphasized.
- God is always waiting for you to return to Him and approach Him with confidence *even* if you don't feel worthy of His love.
- Recognize mistakes, genuinely ask God for forgiveness, learn from them, and get back to growing in your relationship with Him. Rely on God's Grace and Mercy constantly.
- God separates us from our sins as far as the east is from the west (which never meet) and
- God forgives and forgets our sins (Psalm 103:10-14; Hebrews 8:12).

## Sport Application

- Do not allow an error on the field to cause you to feel less than who you are. You are not your performance. Keep them separate. Errors will happen. Get back to the next pitch.
- There's no profit to mentally beating yourself up. God's not doing it. Why should you?

"Well, perhaps you don't know Paul's whole story, or should I say Saul."

"He had two names?"

"More like two lives. Saul was his Hebrew name and Paul was his Greek name. He spent his entire youth dedicated to excelling in the Judean religion to become a Pharisee, which would be like you dedicating your life to becoming a Major Leaguer. Let's read a brief summary in Philippians of him recalling his former religious accomplishments in Judaism:

> Philippians 3:5-6 [NASB]
> [5] circumcised the eighth day, of the nation of Israel, of the tribe of Benjamin, a Hebrew of Hebrews; as to the Law, a Pharisee;
> [6] as to zeal, a persecutor of the church; as to the righteousness which is in the Law, found blameless.

"His resume made him a very valuable player in the Judean religion. In baseball we'd call him a 5-tool player from a Hall of Fame background," Mack related.

"For some reason I thought he was always a Christian but I guess not." I added.

Mack started flipping pages, "Hold your finger there and turn to Acts, where we'll see just how committed Paul was to Judaism before becoming Christian. We'll get a glimpse of Saul in his prime as a Pharisee where he approves the death of a Christian named Stephen for believing on the name of Jesus Christ.

Acts 7:58-8:3[WT]

58After they had cast *him* out of the city, they stoned *him*. The witnesses also laid down their cloaks at the feet of a young man named Saul,

59and they stoned Stephen, who called out and said, "Lord Jesus, receive my spirit."

60Kneeling down, he cried out with a loud voice, "Lord, lay not this sin against them." After he had said this, he fell asleep.

8:1Now Saul approved of his [*Stephen's*] *being put to* death, and in that day, there arose a great persecution against the church that *was* at Jerusalem. All [*in the church at Jerusalem*], except the apostles, were scattered throughout the regions of Judea and Samaria.

²Devout men also carried Stephen *to his burial* and mourned for him greatly.

³However, Saul ravaged the Church. Entering into every house and dragging *out* both men and women, he committed *them* to prison.

"So wait, Paul, or I guess Saul, was a serious enemy of Christianity having them killed and imprisoned?  Are you sure it's the same guy?"

"Same guy," Mack replied.  "Saul thought he was doing the will of God by having Christians killed and persecuting the Church.  Let's see where it all turned around for him:

Acts 9:1-6<sup>WT</sup>

¹Now, Saul, who was still breathing threat and murder against the disciples of the lord, went to the high priest

²and requested from him epistles to the synagogues at Damascus, so that if he found any

who were of the way (both men and women), he could bring *them* bound to Jerusalem.

³As he journeyed, it came to pass that he was approaching Damascus, and suddenly a light from heaven flashed around him.

⁴Falling upon the ground, he heard a voice saying to him, "Saul, Saul, why are you persecuting me?"

⁵Then he said, "Who are you, lord?" And he {+ the lord said}: "I am Jesus whom you are persecuting.

⁶"So rise up and enter the city, and it will be told to you what you must do."

"Jesus Christ *himself* called out to him from heaven?" I asked.

"That's right.  God and Jesus Christ were probably the only ones who could look past what Saul was currently doing to see the potential he held for doing God's *true* work with the same intensity," Mack stated.

"Talk about being good scouts.  I bet Paul would've won comeback player of the year in Bible times.  He had all the potential and it sounds like he just needed a little direction," I said with a smile.

"I agree. He ended up turning his life around and became as committed to spreading the gospel of Christ to the world as he had previously done in wreaking havoc on the Church. And we already know what he did for Christianity once he started his ministry. Pretty incredible example."

"Now *that's* an identity change. But how could he have made such a huge turnaround so quickly?" I asked, pretty sure I would've been full of guilt and shame if I was him.

"He saw Christ's grace bigger than he saw his past life.[94] If Jesus Christ wasn't beating him up over his past, he decided he wouldn't either. And heck, if Jesus Christ told you to do something, wouldn't you go all out for him, too?" Mack asked rhetorically.

"Of course I would. But that's like playing your whole career with the Red Sox and signing with the Yankees. The Red Sox fans who used to love you now hate you and the Yankee fans who used to hate you would be skeptical until you proved yourself!" I joked. "How did Paul deal with it all?"

---

[94] **1 Timothy 1:12-14 WT**: [12]I am thankful to Christ Jesus, our Lord, who made me strong, because he considered me *to be* faithful and put me in the ministry [13]even though I was formerly a slanderer and a persecutor and an abusive person. However, I obtained mercy because I did *it* in unbelief when I was ignorant. [14]So the grace of our lord increased exceedingly with believing and love that *is* in Christ Jesus.

That got Mack laughing. "I like what you did there. And you're right – it wasn't ever easy for Paul after that. The Judean leaders tried to kill or imprison him every chance they got and the Christians understandably were skeptical at first.[95] If you still have your finger in Philippians, let's flip back and we'll find out how Paul was able to leave his former accomplishments in the Judean religion behind and move forward in his *Christ-in* identity.

> Philippians 3:7-9[WT]
>
> [7]However, whatever *things* were gain to me, these have I considered loss for Christ.
>
> [8]I certainly do consider all *those things* to be a loss for the excelling *nature* of the knowledge of Christ Jesus my lord. For him, I sustained the loss of all *those things* (and I consider *them* to be refuse) so that I could gain Christ
>
> [9]and be found in him not having my own justness which *was* of the law but which *is* through believing concerning Christ, the justness from God by the [*right way of*] believing.

---

[95] See Acts 9:10-20

"Jacoby, most people don't realize what Paul was willing to give up as a Pharisee. He had reached the pinnacle of the Judean religion with all its benefits, yet he was willing to throw it all away in order to pursue a greater knowledge of Jesus Christ. He realized that everything he'd accomplished in the world amounted to nothing because it went against pursuing the *true* things of God."

I considered how difficult it must've been to give all that up and wondered if I'd be willing to do the same. My baseball identity had made me the most popular kid in school, the girls liked me and the teachers gave me more breaks in the classroom than most students. "That would've taken some real commitment to leave all that behind and take on a completely new identity knowing it wasn't a popular move."

"Very true. He must have seen greater value in pursuing the things of God than the things of man," he responded.

"I guess that makes sense. If our real identity is in Christ and it's him we represent, it might be a good idea to learn about his life as the example to grow into."[96]

---

[96] **Ephesians 4:11-15 NIV®:** [11]So Christ himself gave the apostles, the prophets, the evangelists, the pastors and teachers, [12]to equip his people for works of

**"True commitment is not necessarily comfortable for you or those around you**. But as you grow in your knowledge of Jesus Christ, you might conclude the same and put your athletic self in the back seat to your Christian identity. Let's skip ahead a few verses as he continues to describe how he moved forward in his *new* identity:

> Philippians 3:13-15<sup>WT</sup>
>
> <sup>13</sup>Brothers, I do not consider myself to have won, but *this* one *thing I do*: Forgetting the *things* that are behind and stretching forward toward the *things* that are ahead,
>
> <sup>14</sup>I press on in pursuit toward the goal for the prize of the upward calling of God in Christ Jesus.
>
> <sup>15</sup>Let us, therefore, as many as *are* mature, think in this manner, and if you do think in any other manner, God will also reveal this to you.

---

service, so that the body of Christ may be built up <sup>13</sup>until we all reach unity in the faith and in the knowledge of the Son of God and become mature, attaining to the whole measure of the fullness of Christ. <sup>14</sup>Then we will no longer be infants, tossed back and forth by the waves, and blown here and there by every wind of teaching and by the cunning and craftiness of people in their deceitful scheming. <sup>15</sup>Instead, speaking the truth in love, we will grow to become in every respect the mature body of him who is the head, that is, Christ.

"Paul was able to move past his former identity by forgetting his past accomplishments and shortcomings and strive for the prize of God's calling in Christ Jesus. Do you remember a couple weeks ago when we talked about eternal rewards?"

"How could I forget?"

"Well, Paul was well aware of them, too. Let's read what God had Paul write down about himself at the end of his life in his second letter to Timothy:

> 2 Timothy 4:6-8[WT]
>
> [6]As a matter of fact, I am already being poured out, and the time of my departure has arrived.
>
> [7]I have contended in the good contest. I have finished the race. I have kept the [*right way of*] believing.
>
> [8]Henceforth, there is reserved for me the crown of justness, which the lord, the just judge, will repay to me in that day, and not only to me but also to all those who have loved his appearing."

I sat there in awe reading what God had Paul write down about himself. Here *I* was thinking I'd be proud to be remembered for throwing a perfect game or making it to the

Bigs.  Yet, in the big-picture perspective of eternity God's opinion of me seems *a little more* important.  "I'm beginning to understand why Paul put his old life behind him and devoted his life to the *true* things of God.  Paul saw the bigger picture and understood the eternal impact he was making, not just a temporary one."

"The greatest commitments in life result in the greatest rewards.  **Few people are willing to make the sacrifices that true commitment requires, but those that do never regret it**.  Jesus Christ was committed to giving his life and look at his reward – God raised him from the dead and gave him a name above every name to which one day every knee will bow.[97]  We also just read that Paul didn't regret fighting the good fight and he's got a crown of righteousness waiting for him in that day Christ returns for us, and there's one for anyone else who patiently anticipates his return, too.  Including us."

I sat back and closed my eyes, imagining what that will be like when Jesus Christ returns to gather the believers, and I

---

[97] **Philippians 2:9-11 WT**:  [9]Wherefore God also highly exalted him and graciously gave him a name that *is* above every name [10]so that in the name of Jesus every knee is to bow, of *those* in heaven and of *those* on the earth and of *those* underground [*buried*], [11]and that every tongue is to confess that Jesus Christ *is* lord to the glory of God, the Father.

saw the end goal – me with a crown of righteousness having fought the good fight of believing and having stood faithful throughout this life for the One True God.

Mack broke the silence. "I remember when I came back from injury, the way I kept from falling back into my old athletic identity was by continuing to make God's image of me *my* image of me and God's standard of living *my* standard of living. In no way was I perfect but I just kept working at it. It also helped to remember the peace of mind that came from no longer caring what others thought of me."

How nice that must feel. I had lived my life and career trying to please everyone and ended up pleasing no one, including myself. Maybe there *was* a freedom in my *Christ-in* identity that the world couldn't offer or touch.

He continued, "It's interesting to think that we've got what, maybe 70 or 80 years on this earth to make an impact? That's nothing compared to eternity. To be remembered and recognized throughout eternity for the work you chose to do for God in the here and now will far outweigh any temporary recognition, even the baseball Hall of Fame."

When I held the perspective of eternity in mind, nothing could hold a candle to God's eternal praise. "I might as well strive for both! I would love for God to say those things about me that he said about Paul at the end of his life."

"I truly believe that by striving first and foremost for God's glory you'll put yourself in the best position to arrive in the baseball Hall of Fame, too," he said.

"Do you really think that *I* could make that big of an impact on baseball and the world for God?"

"Obviously there's no telling in baseball what will happen for you but a large part of it will come down to your level of commitment. And there's no greater commitment you could make than a commitment to God's Word. We already saw what Jesus Christ and the Apostle Paul were able to accomplish in their lifetimes when they got committed."

"That's true. And after seeing the Apostle Paul make that kind of comeback for Christ and immense impact on the world, I'm convinced there's no one God couldn't love and work with in doing incredible things for Him," I concluded.

At that moment Mack had realized time was up and signaled that he'd walk me out. "I agree. God had a good purpose in placing Paul's example in His Word for us of a man who *had it all* by the world's standards but was way in left field when it came to the *true* riches of having a relationship with

Him and choosing pursuits that have an eternal impact. I'll leave you with this from the Apostle Paul:

> Galatians 2:20 [KJV]
>
> I am crucified with Christ; nevertheless I live; yet not *I*, but Christ liveth in me: and the life which I now live in the flesh I live by the faith of the Son of God, Who loved me, and gave Himself for me.

"He counted himself dead to self and alive to Christ. That's commitment. **Remember, people who make the greatest commitments make the greatest impact and earn the greatest rewards**. God will never ask you to change who you are. He'll only encourage you *to be* who He's made you to be in Christ. It's your privilege and responsibility to remind yourself in the mirror each day to see what God sees in you and rise up to believe it. Choose to see the Christ in you!"[98]

---

[98] **Colossians 1:27-29 NIV®:** [27]To them God has chosen to make known among the Gentiles the glorious riches of this mystery, which is Christ in you, the hope of glory. [28]He is the one we proclaim, admonishing and teaching everyone with all wisdom, so that we may present everyone fully mature in Christ. [29]To this end I strenuously contend with all the energy Christ so powerfully works in me.

## Checking for Understanding and for Teaching Others

- When feeling like you can't make a comeback for Christ, ask yourself, *compared to whom*? The Apostle Paul who had Christians imprisoned and killed?

- Paul counted all his personal glory and past accomplishments a loss and gaining a greater knowledge of Jesus Christ and pursuing the things of God his biggest win.

- Paul was so committed to Christ that he counted his own self dead and living inside him was Christ.

- Paul fought the good fight of believing and there's a crown of righteousness reserved for him in that day that Christ returns and for anyone else who looks forward to Christ's return.

## Sport Application

Commitment requires sacrifice and devotion of your whole self. What separates those who make it from those who don't has to do with a sold-out commitment to excellence in every aspect of life. It starts in the preparation and ends in the evaluation. It goes into the little decisions made on a moment-by-moment basis of what you'll choose to entertain and retain in your mind, which then dictates your thoughts and actions.

Sold out commitment will make others uncomfortable. Do it anyway. The most limiting word in the English language is *but*. I am willing to work out, *but* not in the morning. I am willing to work hard in practice, *but*.... Don't allow the word *but* to hold you back from greatness.

Many athletes like the idea of living a life for Christ. But how many truly do it? It's one thing to say you do but another to actually live it day in and day out. Be a doer.

When you truly commit to your mission or the task immediately in front of you, you gain a singular focus free from distractions. True commitment requires sacrifice. What you'll sacrifice in personal glory now doesn't compare to the glory God will shower on you for eternity for standing for Him today. **In life you'll choose to commit yourself to one of two things: Jesus Christ or something else.**

# Patient Endurance

## Chapter 8

It was two days before I was set to leave for summer school and I was nearly finished packing when I received an unexpected phone call from my new head coach. He was calling to tell me he had taken a job with a Major League organization, which meant a new coach would be replacing him and my scholarship would not be honored. He ended the call by letting me know he had put in a good word with some local junior colleges since it was too late to accept an offer at another University.

Two months ago my future had been about as bright as an 18-year-old could dream of and now I couldn't imagine a worse situation. First the injury, then the draft, and now *this*! This wasn't how it was all supposed to play out.

Walking into Mack's office for our final session there was no hiding the disappointment, as he detected it right away. I shared with him the conversation I had with my coach and how I'd lost my scholarship. We sat in silence for what felt like an eternity while Mack digested the situation and I tried pulling myself together.

"I'm really sorry to hear about that, Jacoby," he empathized. "I know how much you were looking forward to leaving in a few days with a fresh start."

"I don't get it," I said in confusion and anger. "I've done everything right and now I've lost everything I worked so hard for."

"Have you prayed about this yet?"

Even after working with Mack the entire summer it still hadn't dawned on me to go to God in prayer in these moments of uncertainty. My mind had gone straight to the doubts, worries, and fears without me ever thinking to slow down, get quiet and pray. "I haven't. Can you pray for me, Mack?"

"Of course," Mack assured me as he reached his hand out to hold mine. "Heavenly Father, we sure love You. We are thankful for all You do in our lives. How you watch over and protect us and guide us. How You heal our hearts and desire nothing more than to have a relationship with us and show Yourself strong on our behalf. God, we're so thankful for the work of Your Son Jesus Christ, who died and rose again that we might have life and have it more abundantly and who made it available for us to approach You with openness and boldness knowing You delight in hearing and answering our prayers. At this time, God, I pray for Jacoby's life and pray that You would comfort and quiet his heart. I also bring his new school situation before you and pray that you would open doors for him to end up at a school that will give him the best opportunity to learn, live, and give his utmost in life, school and baseball. It's with a confident expectation that we bring our prayer requests before you this day and it's in Your Son's name we pray. Amen."

"Amen," I repeated beginning to feel at peace and a bit more hopeful already. "Thanks, Mack. That means a lot to me."

"Glad to do it and I'll keep it in prayer until it gets answered. God's already working on it so stay instant in prayer and be looking at schools you might be interested in," Mack instructed.

I always admired that about Mack. He never got rattled. He just goes to God. I'd miss our time together no matter where I ended up. "Is there an example in the Bible of someone having to deal with a lot of adversity?"

Mack grabbed his Bible off the shelf in excitement as I reached under my seat for mine. "Plenty. But one in particular comes to mind that I think you'll appreciate. It's one of my favorite accounts and it starts out with a boy about your age named Joseph who was the youngest of 12 brothers. God had given him revelation in two separate dreams that one day he'd rise to a position of power and that his family would one day bow down to him."

"I bet his brothers weren't too excited to hear that."[99]

"Not at all. After that they decided they'd had enough of him, so they faked his death and sold him into slavery, where he was bought by a high-ranking official in Pharaoh's army named Potiphar."[100] Mack looked up at me and said, *"I'd call that some adversity."*

---

[99] **Genesis 37:3-5 NIV®**: [3]Now Israel loved Joseph more than any of his other sons, because he had been born to him in his old age; and he made an ornate robe for him. [4]When his brothers saw that their father loved him more than any of them, they hated him and could not speak a kind word to him. [5]Joseph had a dream, and when he told it to his brothers, they hated him all the more.
[100] **Genesis 37:28 & 31-33 NIV®**: [28]So when the Midianite merchants came by, his brothers pulled Joseph up out of the cistern and sold him for twenty shekels of silver to the Ishmaelites, who took him to Egypt. [31]Then they got Joseph's robe, slaughtered a goat and dipped the robe in the blood. [32]They

"Not the start he was expecting on his road to success, I'm guessing," I said, feeling his pain.

"Probably not. Let's pick up the record in Genesis 39 and see what happened to Joseph after getting sold into slavery:

Genesis 39:1-6a[NIV®]

[1]Now Joseph had been taken down to Egypt. Potiphar, an Egyptian who was one of Pharaoh's officials, the captain of the guard, bought him from the Ishmaelites who had taken him there.
[2]The Lord was with Joseph so that he prospered, and he lived in the house of his Egyptian master.
[3]When his master saw that the Lord was with him and that the Lord gave him success in everything he did,
[4]Joseph found favor in his eyes and became his attendant. Potiphar put him in charge of his household, and he entrusted to his care everything he owned.

---

took the ornate robe back to their father and said, "We found this. Examine it to see whether it is your son's robe." [33]He recognized it and said, "It is my son's robe! Some ferocious animal has devoured him. Joseph has surely been torn to pieces."

$^5$From the time he put him in charge of his household and of all that he owned, the Lord blessed the household of the Egyptian because of Joseph. The blessing of the Lord was on everything Potiphar had, both in the house and in the field. $^6$So Potiphar left everything he had in Joseph's care; with Joseph in charge, he did not concern himself with anything except the food he ate.

"How could Joseph be a slave and still be considered a prosperous man?" I asked.

"What did it say right before that?"

My fingers traced the words to find what Mack was talking about, "It says the Lord was with him...."

"That's right. God considered Joseph a successful man because *He* was with him. Joseph may not have been *free* but within the circumstances he found himself in God took care of him and he rose to second in command only to Potiphar *himself*. He would've had all his needs met and if he was living in Potiphar's house, how bad could that be?" Mack emphasized. "His circumstances may have been less than ideal but his situation inside those circumstances was *prosperous*."

Mack had a point. I couldn't help but think how my original plan hadn't worked out but it didn't limit God's ability to still work in my life to make it the best possible experience.

"Let's keep reading.

Genesis 39:6b-10[NIV®]

[6]...Now Joseph was well-built and handsome,

[7]and after a while his master's wife took notice of Joseph and said, "Come to bed with me!"

[8]But he refused. "With me in charge," he told her, "my master does not concern himself with anything in the house; everything he owns he has entrusted to my care.

[9]No one is greater in this house than I am. My master has withheld nothing from me except you, because you are his wife. How then could I do such a wicked thing and sin against God?"

[10]And though she spoke to Joseph day after day, he refused to go to bed with her or even be with her.

"This section always makes me appreciate Joseph's integrity towards God," Mack said with a look of admiration. "No wonder Potiphar was so confident to entrust all that he had to him. It wasn't Potiphar who Joseph was concerned about sinning against—"

"It was *God*," I interjected.

"Exactly, and you won't believe how he's rewarded for his faithful stand," Mack led on.

"Did Potiphar praise him for his integrity and set him free?"

"I wish. After Joseph continued refusing her offers, she made up a story to her husband that Joseph tried to sleep with *her*.[101] We'll pick it up there:

> <u>Genesis 39:19-20</u>[NIV®]
>
> [19]When his master heard the story his wife told him, saying, "This is how your slave treated me," he burned with anger.

---

[101] **Genesis 39:11-18 ESV®**: [11]But one day, when he went into the house to do his work and none of the men of the house was there in the house, [12]she caught him by his garment, saying, "Lie with me." But he left his garment in her hand and fled and got out of the house. [13]And as soon as she saw that he had left his garment in her hand and had fled out of the house, [14]she called to the men of her household and said to them, "See, he has brought among us a Hebrew to laugh at us. He came in to me to lie with me, and I cried out with a loud voice. [15]And as soon as he heard that I lifted up my voice and cried out, he left his garment beside me and fled and got out of the house." [16]Then she laid up his garment by her until his master came home, [17]and she told him the same story, saying, "The Hebrew servant, whom you have brought among us, came in to me to laugh at me. [18]But as soon as I lifted up my voice and cried, he left his garment beside me and fled out of the house."

²⁰Joseph's master took him and put him in prison, the place where the king's prisoners were confined. But while Joseph was there in the prison,"

"Man, this guy can't catch a break!" I shouted, by now realizing his misfortune clearly trumped mine. "First he gets sold into slavery by his brothers and now he's in prison for doing the right thing?"

Mack could sense my perspective changing in feeling less sorry for myself. "It's crazy to think that even though he was a slave in Potiphar's house he had rebuilt a nice life for himself. Then, he lost it all again. **Talk about some major adversity and a pretty good reason to get angry with God. Yet, it never says once that he was bitter towards God or questioned God's faithfulness.** Not once. Might be something worth keeping in mind. Let's see what happens after he's thrown in prison:

Genesis 39:21-23[ESV®]

²¹But the Lord was with Joseph and showed him steadfast love and gave him favor in the sight of the keeper of the prison.

$^{22}$And the keeper of the prison put Joseph in charge of all the prisoners who were in the prison. Whatever was done there, he was the one who did it.

$^{23}$The keeper of the prison paid no attention to anything that was in Joseph's charge, because the Lord was with him. And whatever he did, the Lord made it succeed.

"That's like the Potiphar situation all over again," I recalled. "God took care of him again!"

"That's right. God wasn't bound by Joseph's new circumstances and Joseph refused to think of himself as a slave when he was a slave or as a prisoner when he was in prison. He remained steadfast in his believing that the revelation God gave in those dreams would come to fruition and he persevered in his believing, even amidst the great adversity he was experiencing."

"If I were him I would've been questioning God by then. I'd feel forgotten. You're telling me he got out of prison and somehow rose to power?"

"Let's find out. After some time had passed, Joseph was instructed to serve Pharaoh's chief butler (cupbearer) and baker who had recently been imprisoned. One night they both had dreams and soon learned that Joseph could interpret them. [102] So Joseph revealed that three days later the chief butler would get his job back and Pharaoh would chop off the baker's head. He only asked that when the chief butler was restored to his position that he remember Joseph and ask Pharaoh to release him. Let's see what happened:

### Genesis 40:20-23[ESV®]

[20]On the third day, which was Pharaoh's birthday, he made a feast for all his servants and lifted up the head of the chief cupbearer and the head of the chief baker among his servants.

[21]He restored the chief cupbearer to his position, and he placed the cup in Pharaoh's hand.

---

[102] **Genesis 40:7-8 & 12-15 ESV®**: [7]So he asked Pharaoh's officers who were with him in custody in his master's house, "Why are your faces downcast today?" [8]They said to him, "We have had dreams, and there is no one to interpret them." And Joseph said to them, "Do not interpretations belong to God? Please tell them to me." [12]Then Joseph said to him, "This is its interpretation: the three branches are three days. [13]In three days Pharaoh will lift up your head and restore you to your office, and you shall place Pharaoh's cup in his hand as formerly, when you were his cupbearer. [14]Only remember me, when it is well with you, and please do me the kindness to mention me to Pharaoh, and so get me out of this house. [15]For I was indeed stolen out of the land of the Hebrews, and here also I have done nothing that they should put me into the pit."

$^{22}$But he hanged the chief baker, as Joseph had interpreted to them.

$^{23}$Yet the chief cupbearer did not remember Joseph, but forgot him.

"Are you serious?" I said as I about lost it. "How could he forget him? I'm not going to lie; you sure picked the right story to make me feel better about my situation. I don't know how much more adversity he could take!"

"He persevered in believing for two more years before he got his big break." Mack replied.

"How'd he get out?"

"While Joseph was still in prison, Pharaoh also had some troubling dreams and when none of the magicians and sorcerers could interpret them, the chief butler finally remembered his mistake in forgetting about Joseph and tells Pharaoh where to find him:

### Genesis 41:14-16 $^{ESV®}$

$^{14}$Then Pharaoh sent and called Joseph, and they quickly brought him out of the pit. And when he had shaved himself and changed his clothes, he came in before Pharaoh.

<sup>15</sup>And Pharaoh said to Joseph, "I have had a dream, and there is no one who can interpret it. I have heard it said of you that when you hear a dream you can interpret it."

<sup>16</sup>Joseph answered Pharaoh, "It is not in me; God will give Pharaoh a favorable answer."

"Even in front of Pharaoh, Joseph still gave God all the credit for his ability," Mack acknowledged.

"What was Pharaoh's dream and was Joseph able to interpret it?" I asked.

"Joseph revealed that his dream represented that God would soon give Egypt seven prosperous years followed by seven years of extreme famine. He also explained how Pharaoh should plan for those seven years of famine, by storing up enough food during the prosperous years to cover for Egypt and for all the surrounding countries which, when they came to buy from them, would make Egypt the wealthiest country in the world. Here's Pharaoh's response to all that:

Genesis 41:37-44<sup>NIV®</sup>

<sup>37</sup>The plan seemed good to Pharaoh and to all his officials.

$^{38}$So Pharaoh asked them, "Can we find anyone like this man, one in whom is the spirit of God?"

$^{39}$Then Pharaoh said to Joseph, "Since God has made all this known to you, there is no one so discerning and wise as you.

$^{40}$You shall be in charge of my palace, and all my people are to submit to your orders.  Only with respect to the throne will I be greater than you."

$^{41}$So Pharaoh said to Joseph, "I hereby put you in charge of the whole land of Egypt."

$^{42}$Then Pharaoh took his signet ring from his finger and put it on Joseph's finger.  He dressed him in robes of fine linen and put a gold chain around his neck.

$^{43}$He had him ride in a chariot as his second-in-command, and people shouted before him, "Make way!"  Thus he put him in charge of the whole land of Egypt.

$^{44}$Then Pharaoh said to Joseph, "I am Pharaoh, but without your word no one will lift hand or foot in all Egypt."

I sat there baffled again at how God can work in any situation to bring His promises to pass. "Joseph went from prison to the second most powerful man in Egypt overnight!"

"Yes, but behind that overnight success was thirteen years of patient endurance in the making. He continued to believe God through incredible adversity from the age of 17 when his brothers sold him into slavery until 30 when he became Pharaoh's right-hand man. It wasn't the road to success he imagined, but he never lost sight of God's faithfulness in each of the circumstances he found himself and knew God was the one causing him to prosper all the way to the top."

Mack had somehow found another fitting example for me to learn from. That morning I had received about the worst news possible, and yet, here I was a few hours later more encouraged than ever about my future. I now had the confidence that God would never leave me at any point of my mission to the top[103] and truly believed God isn't bound by circumstances. "Mack, I guess the only question I have left is,

---

[103] **Hebrews 13:5-6 WT**: [5]Be satisfied with what you have, without avaricious behavior, for He has said, Deuteronomy 31:6: "**I shall never ever leave you and I shall never ever, ever forsake you,**" [6]so that we are confident to say: Psalm 118:6: "**The Lord is my helper. I shall not be afraid. What will man do to me?**"

did Joseph's brothers ever bow to him like he predicted in his dream?"

"They sure did,"[104] he said with a smile. "But of even greater importance, it's no coincidence that wherever Joseph went that *that* place prospered. It's no coincidence that three high-ranking officials were so confident in Joseph's ability that it was only their title that made them higher in authority than Joseph. All those men in positions of power, who by the world's standards *had it all*, saw something in Joseph they knew they didn't have – the spirit of God. And it was *this* one man's patient endurance and believing in God that ended up being the catalyst in Egypt becoming the wealthiest nation in the world. Had Joseph given in to his circumstances or seen himself as less than who God made him to be, he would never have persevered to experience the greatness God had in store for him and later the nation of Israel, which we'll hopefully talk about someday."

"And he always gave God the credit," I remarked as I glanced at the clock and knew our time together had drawn to a close. "I'm so thankful to you for everything you've taught

---

[104] **Genesis 42:6 NIV®**: [6]Now Joseph was the governor of the land, the person who sold grain to all its people. So when Joseph's brothers arrived, they bowed down to him with their faces to the ground.

me. I don't know what God's got in store but I know He's going to meet my needs. I'll be in touch and I doubt this will be the last time we see each other."

Mack got up to shake my hand and gave me a hug before walking me out. "Jacoby, it's been an absolute pleasure working with you and teaching you what I know. Keep in mind that you're already a success because you're God's child and whatever circumstances life brings you, God can and will work with you and provide. And as you continue to work heartily unto the Lord and continue to grow in the wisdom of God's Word, you'll become a very valuable addition to your team and organization at every level. God bless you."

## Checking for Understanding and for Teaching Others

- Joseph's road to success was not what he had in mind but he continued to persevere in his believing for 13 years until God made good on His promise.

- God remained faithful to Joseph in each circumstance and always brought him success.

## Sport Application

- Your path won't necessarily be smooth and it's likely you'll be treated unfairly at times, even when you're doing the *right* thing.

- Your circumstances don't define you. Your relationship with God does.

- Continue to persevere and see adversity as a time to grow in your believing towards God.

- You're only ever one moment from getting the call up – it could be today!

# Want to know what Jacoby does next?

Continue the journey by visiting

## RenewedMindPerformance.com/POHG

# Connect with Ray on Social Media

/RenewedMindPerformance

/RenewedMindRay3

/RenewedMindPerformance

# Keynote Speaking

Si

ar

*Baseball Chapel 2017*

# Team Consulting

Ray consults with teams and coaching staffs to help establish the winning processes that lead to successful results by helping establish team core values, routines, and a common language geared towards building each other up and getting likeminded on the road that leads to victory!

# 1-on-1 Consulting

Work one on one with Ray to individualize your mental skills training program to help you maximize your performance and be a big addition to your team's success!

**Visit RenewedMindPerformance.com to learn more!**

# The mental skills training program that will help you build a Major League Mindset...in just 21 hours!

## Visit **RenewedMindPerformance.com/21HMP** to learn more!

**Kodi Medeiros, 1ˢᵗ Round Draft Pick 2014, Milwaukee Brewers:**

*"I've been working with Ray for about 4 months now and it's been going really well. He's helped me a lot with the mental part of the game especially as I've struggled to pitch with runners on base. Working with Ray has allowed me to execute my pitches effectively with runners on base by accepting the situation and visualizing the runners disappear from the baseline before I pitch. I'm realizing the benefits of growing in the mental game...and you should too!"*

Made in the USA
Middletown, DE
11 September 2017